# The Beginning

Book One in the Series
*Beyond The Voices*

MARY KATHERINE FONTANERO

The Beginning - Book 1 - Beyond the Voices Series
Copyright © 2014 Mary Katherine Fontanero
All rights reserved.

ISBN: 098686885X
ISBN-13: 978-0986868856

# DISCLAIMER

This is a work of fiction. Names, characters, places, and incidents either are the product of the author's imagination or are used fictitiously. Any resemblance to actual persons, living or dead, events, or locales, is entirely coincidental.

# CONTENTS

| | | |
|---|---|---|
| 1 | The Girl | 1 |
| 2 | The Voice | 17 |
| 3 | Accepting the Truth | 42 |
| 4 | Friendship | 54 |
| 5 | Second Chances | 87 |
| 6 | The Opportunist | 103 |
| 7 | Phone Call | 135 |
| 8 | The Path | 158 |
| 9 | Moving Forward | 194 |
| | About The Author | 225 |

**Author's Notes\***

The sound of the voice of the character Magnus, is distinctly different from Tom's. Although not a different language, to Tesh, it's almost indecipherable. He uses the incorrect tense of words and their meaning is as if spoken by one who is unable to grasp the english language.

Rather than make it difficult for the reader, *Magnus's speech is written correctly but depicted by this font.*

# CHAPTER 1
## The Girl

I remember standing at the screen door, the sun shining so bright it made you squint, the row of tall spruce trees moving gently in the wind as if waving like royalty, and the smell of spring in the air. Between the house and the trees, off to the right, was our swing set. The solo rhythmic squeaking of the swing as my brother moved back and forth on his side, tauntingly indicated that mine hung silent and empty. I stood on the other side of the wood framed screen door, crying and begging to join him, refusing to retreat to my Mother's bedroom and nap with her. The rheumatoid arthritis was well established in her ankles and wrists by then. It necessitated she nap at midday to regain enough strength to make dinner for my brother and I, and sometimes our Dad.

Dad was rarely at home, spending most of his life away working on the rigs. We were told it was to pay for the farm because it didn't support itself, but Mom and Dad never really got along all that well so even when he was at home, he worked on various farm projects rather than spending time with Mom. Dad wasn't a big man, but strong from physical work. I remember his large hands and how he would rub them with oil when they were rough and dry after a day's work on the farm. His hair was dark, his skin tanned brown like leather, and when he removed his hat, he exposed a pale white forehead. He wore dark framed glasses and had a gold capped canine tooth that was visible when he smiled.

Mom was a smoker. It seemed to be one of the few pleasures she had in life with her limited mobility. There were photos in the storage chest in the attic of her when she was younger. Her hair was blond and wavy, her legs slim and muscled. She stood tall and healthy, not crouched over and pained as I remember.

On more than one occasion I remember asking Mom if she and Dad loved one another. Her response was always the same and I thought it odd that she included my brother and I in her answer.

"People show their love in different ways, Hunny. It's not always like what you see in those movies you watch on TV. Of course he loves us."

I always wished Dad would have been more romantic toward Mom anyway, but I would later learn that she was treated better than many others in our community. I don't have any memories of him hugging her or even speaking lovingly towards her. Their conversation was logistical and superficial. When he would leave us, he would lean his cheek toward each of us, including Mom, allowing us to kiss him good-bye. Loving words were not part of his vocabulary, but I knew that despite his tough exterior there was a softness inside and a sense of responsibility toward us that never wavered. There was always food on the table and although we weren't spoiled, we didn't want for anything either. Dad was a good provider, and Mom was Mom. Rest their souls.

I had brought a manila envelope full of old photos to the office and on days like today, would pick through them during my lunch break, separating ones to add to an album cataloguing my youth. This labor of love had been dragging on for months, but was a welcome distraction to the hectic pace of the office with its' endless flow of patients and inevitable office issues. I had come across a photo from the day on the swing and by looking at my age, thought it was probably my first memory of my childhood. There I was, on the swing set with my brother, red sweatshirt, knit red toque tied beneath my chin and blue corduroy pants tucked into black rubber boots with orange soles. My hair was a mess of blond waves randomly visible beneath the red toque. I noticed the well-spaced little white teeth in my open mouth and light green eyes dancing with joy. The sun was indeed shining and patches of brown grass, dirty with gravel were visible, but the red chubby fingers grasping the chains of the swing and pink hue on our cheeks and noses proved spring had barely arrived. A clear smudge across the red sleeve of the sweatshirt was a sure sign I'd wiped my nose without using the tissue that would have been tucked up my left sleeve. My brother wore a navy raincoat, green and blue striped toque with his jeans tucked into a pair of boots identical to mine. We were both laughing and enjoying one of the first warm days. It would have been nearly impossible to keep a strong willed youngster inside after a long, cold winter. I don't remember how I finally got the freedom to go out that day, but the photo, now in my album, is a bitter sweet reminder of how, at the ripe old age of about three, I was already mastering the techniques needed to get what I wanted.

My brother, Johnny, was three years older than I. His hair was almost white blonde, his soft brown eyes shone gentle and kind. He had beautiful straight white teeth and a smile that melted hearts. I remember watching him gently hugging our Mom not wanting to cause her more pain than the arthritis was already inflicting upon her. Johnny more than made up for what Dad lacked in affection, especially when it came to Mom.

We lived 4 miles from town, a vast expanse as kids, and although we played well together for the most part, there were times of unrest when one's imagination became a tool to create a world of wonder and magic. Photos in my album document some of those days. There's one of me at about six years with a bouquet of flowers, yellow, similar to a buttercup, but different because of their shiny round lily pad like leaves. I remember late spring and wandering through the swampy flood plain next to the river once the water had receded back into its banks. The Marsh Marigolds scattered throughout made the stunning yellow bouquet for the supper table, but wilted and dropped their petals before the next morning when removed from their cool, wet bed at the base of the trees. It was during those times I pretended to be lost in a dense unfamiliar forest, gathering flowers in an attempt to sooth my frightened soul. I'd eventually be rescued by a handsome prince of course and safely returned to the confines of my castle and courtyard where I was to stay for my own protection. The forest was a dangerous place for a beautiful princess.

At other times, my brother and I would spend the afternoon draining puddles into one another by etching troughs with the garden tools. We'd create small lakes and build villages using rocks and sticks, each of us trying to outdo the other, stealing ideas through quick glances and then boasting, "look at mine!" The ice that formed on the little rivers and lakes during the cold night shattered beneath our rubber boots the next morning as we stomped like giants invading one another's peaceful settlements. The garden was another story. There the water and mud would suck your boots off and leave you standing with one foot in cold mud and the other buried inside a submerged boot if you tried to walk from one side of the garden to the other. It was as irresistible as crushing someone else's little village of sticks and stones.

My album contains many photos, almost a decade, of me with my horses. As I grew older, my interest in mud puddles and swings had changed to horses and boys. As I look back at the photos today, I can better understand why my mother was so adamant about my having a horse. My hair was now long and wavy, the sandy blond colour unchanged except for sun bleached streaks throughout. Faded blue jeans and t-shirts were my daily uniform then. Black rubber boots had been replaced by dark brown Ariat roper boots, and my teeth were white and straight like my brother's now. Mom always insisted I had horses and although we had other animals on the farm, the horses were my responsibility. This wasn't so for Johnny, and I now believe her reason for keeping me busy was more about keeping me away from the boys than anything. What she didn't realize, however, was my horse actually allowed me to get to the boys. By the time I was twelve years old I would ride bareback beyond the familiar surroundings near our small hobby farm, across neighbouring fields and river crossings, and past the big working farms belonging to Johnny's friends. As long as I avoided the tender fields of wheat, I was free to ride until it was time to return for dinner and homework. I was often farther away from home than I should have been at that age, imagining that if I continued to search, I would one day find my prince, my happily ever after. As long as I can remember, there was an emptiness, a need I felt, but had no idea how to satiate. I always wanted more than where I was or what I had.

"Tesh, you have patients waiting in both examining rooms," Carol's gentle but urging voice jolts me back to reality. I gather up the photos and pack it all away into my bike pannier before beginning my afternoon roster of patients.

"Hello Kathy," I greet my first patient, "How have you been feeling? Sit up here and I'll check your blood pressure."

"Well, I'm not great actually. I'm so stressed with the business, its 24/7 and more than I can handle."

"I see. Are you still walking every day? Your weight is up a little and I'm not satisfied with the triglyceride and LDL levels," I say as I note her blood pressure and look through the lab work."

"Yes, I'm walking most days, and trying to stay on a diet. I started drinking fruit shakes for breakfast."

"Fruit shakes are often worse for us than a poached egg on toast because of the sugar content. That might be why you've gained a few pounds, Kathy. I'll ask Carol to provide you with our list of recommended websites, which can really help with weight loss if you stay the course. We'll increase the medication for your cholesterol and I'll see you in a month. Keep walking, it will help relieve some of that stress, too."

I move steadily between one of three rooms until the last patient has been seen. My work day ends after another hour of dictation as Carol walks by my office.

"See you in the morning Doc!"

"You bet, Carol. That was a busy day. Thanks for keeping us on time."

I thank my lucky stars for my nurse Carol who makes the busiest of days manageable as I head to the bathroom to change into my cycling gear and throw some cold water on my face before the ride home. As I stand over the sink with the tap water running, I become aware of how many memories have been stirred by the old photos. Splashing cold water on my face reminds me of days at the swimming hole as a kid.

"Can I come, too, Johnny?" I begged.

"Why can't you do something with your friends and leave mine alone?" he replied with a familiar retort.

"Well even if I had a friend over I wouldn't be allowed to go to the river with them. Mom won't let us. Pleeeeease Johnny."

Now Johnny knew he should give in at that point or he'd risk not being allowed to go at all if Mom heard him. It wasn't so much that she thought he should take me along as much as it was an opportunity for her to rest without having to listen to my complaining that I didn't have a friend over. Johnny had several that lived close by and they rode their bikes back and forth. There were no girls close to my age within my limited walking distance so if I didn't join in with the farm boys, I was on my own.

"Okay, get ready then. We're meeting them at the swimming hole. Don't make me wait for you," he gave in at last and directed as he stormed out, allowing the screen door to slam shut behind him.

"Mom, I'm going swimming with Johnny and the boys," I yelled a few minutes later as I ran out of the house and across the yard before she had a chance to respond, swimsuit rolled up in a towel and tucked up underneath my arm.

My heart was pounding with excitement already, and it wasn't just because I loved swimming or that this would be one of the first swims of the season, I wanted to be around the boys more than I cared to have a friend over to ride my horses. The swimming was indeed fun and the boys even threw the football to me a couple of times, which was surprising as in past years, they usually just ignored me. I was always within earshot and could listen to how they talked to one another about swimming, cars, trucks, sports and girls.

"Dad let me drive to town yesterday and we followed a cop car all the way there," Johnny bragged.

"In the truck? They never pull anyone over in a work truck. That's a sure way to piss the farmers off," Daren assured them.

"Did you see the game last night?" interjected Kevin, who was a big baseball fan.

They didn't talk about girls their own age, not wanting to venture into unfamiliar territory or be teased if they let on they liked one of them, but they talked at length about magazine models and movie stars.

"She's nice, but I prefer brunettes."

"I used to think that, but not anymore. I like blondes now after seeing Bo's spread."

My brother liked Bo Derek with her beaded and cornrow braided hair. He referred to her in Playboy magazine as often as he could saying she looked better in a bikini than a one piece. I silently agreed as I'd discovered the magazine one rainy afternoon while looking through comics underneath Johnny's bed.

"I'm cold. I'm gonna change and just watch." I told my brother after an hour or so in the muddy cold water of our swimming hole. The boys were all shivering, too, but none seemed ready to leave the swinging rope that hung from a large poplar tree at the edge of the river. There were three other boys besides Johnny. Kevin Long was a year younger than my brother, dark haired and tall with skin that tanned to a deep brown. He was the oldest of four kids and had a maturity and sensibility about him different from the others. I noticed he was always watching me, but I think it was more from habit of watching out for his younger siblings than his being interested in me. Ben Douglas, who was the same age as Johnny, 15 years at that time, was strong from picking hay bales from the fields and stacking them neatly in the barn for their large herd of cattle. He had brown hair and a nose that appeared too large for his face. Ben was the same height as my brother, and was quiet when his older brother, Daren, was around. Daren was only a year older, but at 16, he dwarfed the boys in personality and confidence. They listened intently when he talked about high school dances and his Lance Romance experiences which I learned later were mostly exaggerated. Daren wore faded blue jeans and let his dirty blond hair grow a little longer than the others. I thought he was the greatest.

I made my way back toward the boys at the swimming hole, listening to their laughter and name calling and I suspected they were snapping their wet towels at each other. As I rounded the thick caragana bush to witness their usual antics, I was surprised to see they hadn't yet put all their clothes back on. Rather than lowering my eyes, I stood frozen in place, looking at four naked boys fighting one another with their towel whips.

"Tessy!" someone yelled and they quickly covered themselves. In the flurry that followed, I noticed Ben seemed less embarrassed than the others about what I'd witnessed that day. He was the only one that spoke to me on our way to the main road from the river.

"Tessy, next time you ride by the farm, stop in and I'll saddle up Blaze and go for a ride with ya."

I smile as I recall those carefree days, dry my face, pack my work clothes in the bike pannier alongside the old photos, and guide the bike down the back steps to the street. The late afternoon air is warm as I begin the ride home. I feel a familiar surge of freedom as I pick up speed along the designated bike lane that winds its' way through the less busy downtown streets to the outlying residential neighbourhoods. My commute time on the bike is about the same as in my car, 20 minutes, but I find the short ride allows me to clear my head and relax for the evening.

The town-home is welcoming and quiet at first, but as I step further inside I'm greeted by Rex, our orange tabby cat. She meows as she brushes past my legs, flops on the floor in front of me and stretches her body in a half moon shape waiting for her belly to be rubbed. She wasn't always this loving, but eventually realized her life was better here than behind the dumpster at the back of the Rexall pharmacy, hence the dog name. Tom and I had bumped into one another that day, me on my bike and him in his truck. We pulled over behind a strip mall to talk and while we were standing there, we heard meowing that seemed to be coming from beneath a dumpster. Tom was covered with grease and grime, saying he hadn't been this dirty since his days as a mechanic, but had managed to squeeze behind the garbage container and rescue a dirty little frightened orange kitten. His hands were covered in scratches, and after we'd taken her to the vet for shots and a cleanup, she disappeared underneath our bed. I tried to coax her out with every treat and toy imaginable and when Tom finally convinced me to ignore her, she started to appear more and before long, became a "pest" as Tom called her.

I make a cup of tea with milk, the way my Mom did, and toast a piece of Tom's latest bread creation made in the recently purchased bread maker, another good reason to ride to and from work every day. Rex jumps up beside me on the love seat as I flip through the local paper. She seems determined to have my attention tonight, stretching her paws across the paper and pushing her head into my hand. After a few moments of her antics, I abandon my paper and rub her belly until she stretches out to her full length, closes her eyes and starts to purr. It makes me smile to see how much she thrives on the affection and I speak to her as if she were human.

"We're so much the same, Rexxy. It's all about the love isn't it?"

With those words serving as a reminder, I find myself looking back on the night that Tom entered my life. I've replayed those memories in my head again and again, those early days and nights, the ones that changed my life forever. For it is from here that the real story begins.

# CHAPTER 2
## The Voice

It was three years ago this month that I met Tom. I had stopped at my regular cafe, cleverly named *Witch Brew?*, at the end of a particularly difficult day. As I sat at one of the corner tables blankly staring into my cup, I wondered how we would ever get out of the mess we were in now. I couldn't make sense of what Ken had done with our finances and how he believed by continuing, it would eventually get better. The series of sleepless nights and mind numbing days was taking their toll on my health as I struggled to get through to Ken. If we made changes now we might be able to salvage my practice at least. It was a few moments before I noticed someone was standing at my table and I looked up through bleary eyes to see him.

"Hhhello," I stammered, surprised to see the seemingly shy man who was here most mornings queued up with the rest of us for our various cups of addiction. Most regulars were pleasant to one another and even chatted while waiting their turn. He, however, seemed to ignore me and everyone else, barely smiling or speaking. It had become a bit of a game to see if I could engage him in a greeting or even a smile. Tonight, however, he seemed different.

"May I join you?"

Before I could answer he sat down on the opposite side of the table, smiled warmly, and began speaking.

"I'm Tom. I heard the talkative ones call you Tesh. This would be your name?"

I nodded in agreement, too stunned to speak.

"By the looks of you, you've put in a long day without a lot of rest or food. And as someone in your position knows, it's important to eat." With that he pushed a plate of fruit and sliced granola bar toward me and motioned that I should eat. I reached for a strawberry, wondering how he knew I hadn't eaten all day.

As he talked, I found myself relaxing, his voice was soothing. I picked at the granola bar and sipped my latte. I struggle now to remember the conversation, all I really remember was the feeling of calm that came over me as he spoke.

"Are you finished?" he asked.

"Yes," I replied.

Then he looked at me and in a strange voice said, "*because I knew you hadn't eaten.*"

I stared at him for a moment, nodded and stood up.

"Let's go then. Put this on." He handed me his jacket and stepped toward the door, opened it for me, and I walked over to where my bike was locked. I placed the key for the bike lock in his outstretched hand, and with a shiver swung the jacket over my shoulders.

"You are in no shape to ride now. I'll drive you home, Tesh," and with that he gently loaded the bike into the back of his truck, opened the passenger door and closed it behind me. I gave him directions to the furnished town-home I'd rented just days prior. Few words passed between us other than those necessary to navigate the road home, unusual for people who barely knew one another and yet I don't remember feeling uncomfortable at all. He parked the truck on the street and unloaded my bike. Once in the cool night air, I became acutely aware of the large decaf latte that was now stretching my bladder to capacity. I opened the front door and quickly slipped out of my cycling shoes as he leaned my bike against the wardrobe box in the entrance.

"Make yourself at home, Tom. I have to use the washroom."

"Thank you for not doing that in my truck," he teased as he watched me bolt for the bathroom door.

"Whew!" I said a few minutes later as I opened the bathroom door, and noticed Tom was sitting on one of the tall stools at the kitchen counter with his back facing me. I started speaking as I walked towards him, wondering how I might end the evening without being rude.

"Thanks for the ride home, Tom. I might not have made it riding with that latte on board." As I was coming around to face him, Tom grabbed onto my wrist and pulled me close enough that his mouth was near my ear.

"*Relax now.*" It was the same strange voice I'd heard briefly in the cafe telling me he knew I hadn't eaten today. He gently stroked my arm with his other hand as I tried to collect my thoughts. This wasn't Tom's voice! My stomach lurched and my body stiffened momentarily as I realized something was very different. A tingling feeling started in my scalp, travelled across my shoulders, down both arms and ended once it reached my fingertips. I'd never felt this before; it was as if his words had penetrated right through me.

"*Relax. I'm here now. Everything will be good.*" The voice was somehow more distant, deeper, and some of the words he used didn't really make sense. I listened intently, my mind flooding with thoughts about what might be happening, and what I should do next.

*"You've been confused by your soulmate. He has not been wise and is putting the family in a place that is not good. You would not be doing this on your own my Powerful One."*

"Powerful One?" I asked. I liked the sound of that, but was he referring to me?

*"Yes. That's you,"* he answered.

I could feel my heart pounding in my chest and yet I didn't feel the need to break away and run from the voice that was speaking to me now, not that I thought I could. I'd noticed earlier that Tom was strong with the hands of a man who had worked hard all his life. I wondered how he knew about my situation with Ken. Powerful One? What was happening?

*"I love my Powerful One. I've always loved you. I tried to get to you sooner, but it takes time to do this. I could not get here before this, but everything is good now. I have you here now."* He continued to caress my arm, shoulder, head and the side of my face as he spoke and although his speech was broken and difficult to understand, I wanted to hear more. It was as if I'd recognized something and as odd as it seemed at the time, I was connecting to it. He continued to reassure me with gentle, loving words and I began to relax. As he spoke, he released the hand that was holding my wrist and used it to cradle my back and soothe me with his touch. In fact, I was surprised as I started to feel aroused, not just because I was

hearing words I'd yearned to have spoken to me for so long, but because this somehow seemed right. He smelled wonderful, his body was warm and his hands gentle but firm.

*"We will be together now, in the bedroom. We will speak more and I will explain."*

He took my hand and motioned for me to guide us to the bedroom. Once there he began to remove his clothing and I did the same. He laid on his back and lifted his arm for me to lay my head on his shoulder, drawing me closer as I obliged. As I lay there, I couldn't tell if his eyes were open or closed, but I could see there was a silver pentagram-like pendant on the chain I'd noticed earlier around his neck that now lay nestled in the cover of hair on his chest. After a few moments lying together with him continually caressing my arm, shoulder and the side of my face exploring the places he touched as if he were blind and trying to discover what I might look like, he spoke again. *"You may touch the penis of the aerial now."*

"The aerial?" I asked.

*"Yes, this one is the aerial,"* and he placed his hand on his own chest.

*"Get it hard and we will speak. This makes it easier on the aerial when we do this."*

I moved my hand beneath the covers and grasped the soft penis, rhythmically stroking it until it became firm in my hand.

## THE BEGINNING

*"This aerial doesn't know he's with you in this bed. He will not know what we're speaking and doing, he will only know what you're hiding."*

"What? I don't understand. How is it that he won't know what we're talking about or doing, but he'll know something that's hiding? What do you mean hiding?"

*"You will understand these things in time. I cannot tell you what to say. You must be the one speaking it. The aerial will become a friend."*

I was relieved to hear those words even though I didn't completely understand what the voice had said. What must I speak about? Friend?

*"You may put the penis inside you,"* and he took his arm and gently rolled me on top of him. I positioned myself above him, with the end of his penis at the opening of my already wet vagina. As I slowly pushed myself onto him I was suddenly overcome with a profound sense of euphoria, emotion and lust. For a moment I thought I might lose control of my entire being. It had been awhile since I'd had sex and even longer that I didn't know what to do, but this was something I'd never experienced before. The feelings that were surging through me as I gently moved my body back and forth were as close to ecstasy as I have known. Thoughts flooded my mind trying to grasp what I was experiencing. He remained quiet, barely moving other than his hands caressing my hips and

waist, slowly moving up to my breasts and gently squeezing my nipples.

*"How does that feel?"*

"Wonderful. Amazing!"

*"You may touch yourself now."*

How did he know I touch myself? I'd only ever been able to orgasm by touching myself either during intercourse or when I was alone and it was generally only after some time that I felt comfortable enough to do this with a lover. I sat more upright on his penis, wet my finger inside the top of my vagina and began moving it through the slippery wetness next to the now swollen clitoris. I squeezed and relaxed the muscles inside my vagina as I gently rocked back and forth on his penis. Within moments my breathing became more rapid until I held my breath momentarily. I felt warmth inside my body, and shuddered several times as the orgasm released me. As he gently pulled my arms toward him, I let out my breath and folded forward, laying my head on his shoulder and putting my mouth close to his ear. He remained calm, lying almost still, but continued to stroke my head and back.

*"I will not put the juice inside you. Do not worry. You are not ready."*

"Thank you," I replied with a sigh of relief. I was irresponsible not to have enquired earlier about birth control and now felt a stab of guilt for having pleasured myself without him doing the same. I had never been with a man that did not orgasm during sex, ever. And it wasn't until I was in university that I had an orgasm myself. Generally it was me that went without, only to lay awake listening to the sound of heavy breathing and then snoring while the familiar feeling of a lonely emptiness crept slowly over my body, smothering what I'd thought were feelings of mutual pleasure. Throughout my marriage with Ken I rarely achieved orgasm during sex. In the beginning I wasn't comfortable enough to touch myself and as time went on he was less and less interested in my pleasure. His love making was very uncreative and he didn't have the equipment to completely satisfy me. I preferred having him behind me or had to have a pillow underneath my hips so I could at least feel his cock deep enough inside me. I rarely had the pleasure of sucking him off. He didn't seem to want me to give him a blow job nor would he masturbate into my mouth and allow me to swallow his cum. I never understood why he kept those things from me when I was so willing to do whatever I could to pleasure him and myself at the same time.

He continued to rub my body, allowing me to relax until I was almost asleep.

"*I will go now my Powerful One. You rest. We will be together this next day.*"

With that, he rose, dressed and quietly left. I heard the door shut as I was drifting toward sleep. I settled deeper beneath the covers, thought of him cradling my head with one hand and caressing my back with the other, felt another rush of excitement through my body and remember telling myself, now that's what it's like to be loved, Tesh. I slept soundly for the first time in months, waking up eight hours later with the sun beating down on my face through the crack in the drapes.

As I lay in bed slowly waking from my slumber, dread and anxiety about my family situation were not my first thoughts of the day. The reality of what I'd done last night started to hit me. I'm still fucking married! Separated, but just, and isn't my goal to work things out with Ken? What the hell! I'm no better than my married buddies I screwed when I was in medical school! And what about Tom? Is he married? I don't know anything about him. Then I paused in thought. And the voice? With that I started to calm down again, and my thoughts changed from loud disbelief to a quiet whisper. Why had I felt so calm and open to him? It was as if I'd been intoxicated or under some sort of spell, not completely in control of myself. I replayed everything I could remember from the previous evening, the calming voice, the gentle caressing, the odd feeling of familiarity and suddenly I knew I couldn't just lie there all day going over and over this in my mind without it driving me crazy.

I quickly dressed and made my way back to the *Witch Brew?*, hoping he'd be there despite it being Saturday morning and different than the regular weekday routine. I hung around for a half hour, but eventually gave up, stopping at the grocery store to pick up a few things. My heart jumped into my throat when I saw him with a grocery basket in his hand.

"Hi Tom!"

It was as if I'd caught him off-guard, and he nodded without speaking, taking a small step backward.

"I guess we're bound to run into one another around the neighbourhood," I fumbled, remembering what I'd been told last night and feeling awkward and embarrassed. I turned to leave, raising my hand to wave good-bye when I heard the now familiar voice and felt a welcome piercing through my body.

*"I'll be at your home tonight at seven."*

I was so happy to hear those words I wanted to hug Tom, but thought better of it, said goodbye, and left the store without buying anything.

I spent the rest of the day periodically looking at the clock as I unpacked a few personal belongings in an attempt to make the place feel like a home, but as evening drew closer I found I needed a glass of wine to relax. I put my feet up on an unpacked box, rested my head back on the pillows of the overstuffed couch, and took a swallow of wine. The next thing I knew, the doorbell was ringing. I jumped up and rushed to the door without even thinking I might have slobber running down my chin or pillow marks on my face. He entered without looking startled so I knew I was probably okay.

"Thank you for inviting me over for drinks," he commented as he walked inside, handing me a bag and baguette, while holding a bottle of red wine in his other hand.

"Oh, jeez thanks for bringing this, Tom. I got caught up with unpacking and I didn't think to pick anything up."

"I know, I watched you leave the store with an empty grocery basket in your hand," he replied. I laughed and invited him to come in.

We walked into the kitchen and I handed Tom the bottle opener while I retrieved two wine glasses out of the cupboard. He expertly withdrew the cork and poured each of us a glass of wine as I watched, noticing he didn't have any sign of a ring tan on his left hand.

"I remember these places being built," he began and his relaxed demeanour helped calm me as it had the night before in the cafe. "They were just underway after I moved here and I even went through them," Tom continued. "I thought it would be a nice layout."

"Well I haven't been here that long actually, but come to think of it, I find the place pretty convenient overall and spacious feeling," I added.

Tom started to unpack the bag of groceries, passing me the baguette.

"My past experience with you made me think you probably haven't put much thought into food so I brought something to put in your stomach with that wine."

Within minutes he had sliced the aged gouda and spicy sausage placing them on a platter along with a mixture of olives and baguette. We decided to sit on the south facing deck while the sun was still there to keep it warm.

Conversation with Tom was easy. The deck overlooked a public park where people were busy walking their dogs, riding bikes and generally enjoying a warm evening outdoors. Tom would point at a couple and then pretend to be them as they talked and walked. His interpretation of what their conversation might entail had me in stitches. Every once in a while he would point out something unusual like the man with his bike helmet on backward so he could find his way back to where he came from, the lady with her hair and clothing so perfect she must be wound tighter than a top and the couple holding hands but not speaking or smiling the entire time they walked in the park. His observations were insightful and he had a sense of humour about everything he spoke about. I wondered later if this might have been one of the first times in my life that I didn't feel some sort of sexual tension or pressure that there might be an expectation for sex later. Eventually I decided to speak up.

"I've only been separated for a short time, Tom. I hope I haven't given you any wrong impressions about my situation."

"Each day I saw you in line waiting for coffee, I thought you looked like someone who could use a friend, just a friend," he emphasized. "That is my only expectation, Tesh. I don't expect you to say or do or be anything more than that. Next weekend there's a flea market in Colmer that I like to go to. Would you like to join me? Great people watching!"

"Ya, that sounds great," I replied, letting out an audible sigh of relief. I really did need a friend, but more than anything I felt I needed to get my family back together again.

With that, Tom leaned forward.

"*You see now? The aerial is good. You will enjoy his company. We will go to the bedroom.*" He stood up and walked into the house. I followed him to the bedroom and my time with the voice began similar to the night before. He silently removed his clothing and I did the same, then snuggled up beside him as he lay on his back. He held me close, stroked my hair and face.

*"I love my Powerful One. You must stimulate the penis when we speak. Do you understand?"*

"Yes, you want me to stroke the penis while we're speaking."

*"Correct. Tell me about your day."*

"Why do you call me Powerful One?"

*"Because that's who you are,"* he replied as if I should know this.

"You want to hear about my day?" I asked somewhat surprised at the request.

*"Yes, that's what I said."*

I began by telling him about unpacking, and the tasks I had accomplished that day. He listened politely although I sensed he may not understand what I was talking about.

*"I don't understand unpacking,"* he said after my long description about the move to my new place at 100 - 2020 Harbour Way.

Our communication was odd to be kind, his words came in shortened, at times very funny, sentences.

*"What you doodling?"* he'd enquire.

"What am I doodling?" I'd ask.

*"That's what I said."*

I started to giggle.

"*What are you doing?*" he scolded with a humorous edge to his voice. Although I felt he was someone to respect, I was not fearful of him in the least, which was unlike me for I'd spent my entire life being dominated by men.

"I don't mean to be disrespectful, but you make me laugh. I feel good inside," I told him.

"*Only people trying to hide are fearful and not calm,*" he replied. "*Why are you not stimulating?*"

I moved my hand up and down again and thought about what he'd said. My understanding of those words were that only those with something to hide are fearful and not calm. I wondered if I was hiding anything?

"I don't believe I'm hiding anything. Am I ?"

"*Yes, all people hide, mostly from themselves. You are not trying to hide at this time. You are too young to understand these things. I cannot tell you what to say,*" he explained and then hesitated for a moment before speaking again. "*Remember one moon ago?*"

Those words hit me with a jolt. "I wasn't trying to hide the fact I'd had an affair, but I was trying to forget I'd done that."

"*Trying to forget is the same as hiding. Speak of it now.*"

"About a month ago I was out of town at a conference, by myself. I was desperate for sex, for intimacy, for someone to be attracted to me, to pay attention to me and want me. At times I think I would have fucked anybody or anything. It didn't matter. I was horny! I've been this way my whole life. Ken hadn't been interested in me sexually for so long and now we were sleeping in separate bedrooms. I had to beg him to have sex before this and now I had had none for months. He just didn't want to fuck me and I couldn't understand it. Isn't it usually men who want sex and their wives aren't interested? It was eating me up inside and I had convinced myself, as foolish as it sounds now, that if I could find satisfaction outside of my marriage, I could get through until we sorted out our problems. I found what I was looking for within an hour or so of the first evening. He was there on his own, no wedding band and when he started to pay attention to me, I let him know I was there alone, too. We met for drinks in the hotel lounge after the sessions had ended. I had one of my favourite dresses on and felt sexy just sitting across from him. I was wet knowing what was about to happen. When he suggested going for dinner I suggested going to his room instead. We kissed and undressed, both eagerly exploring one another's bodies. I watched as he unzipped his pants and pulled the top of his underwear down to allow his hard cock to escape. My mouth was watering as he lowered his pants and underwear exposing his shaved balls. I immediately went down on my knees and licked them before putting his cock in my mouth. He was a little bigger than Ken which made me even more excited as I anticipated being fucked. When he lifted me up and bent me over the end of the bed, I thought he was going to lick me, but he lay down beside me on the bed and continued to rub my body, telling me how wonderful I looked. I turned myself around, putting my cunt close to his head hoping he might take advantage of the opportunity while I put his cock in my mouth again, but he didn't lick or finger fuck me. His hands went to my breasts and when he started to squeeze my nipples I could feel my juices dripping from inside me. I eventually turned onto my back and he pulled me toward the edge of the bed. I could feel his hard cock pressing on my inner thigh and then against my cunt before it slid inside me. I arched my back and pressed against him as I felt him spreading me apart with his cock. I wanted him to ram it inside me rather than the gently fucking he was giving me. I locked my ankles around his ass, put my hands on the back of his legs and pulled him hard against me telling him to fuck me, but he just didn't seem to understand how I needed to be fucked. Even when I could feel him starting to reach orgasm his rhythm never changed. When he came I pushed him onto his back and started licking him, hoping he'd stay hard and would be able to fuck more, but despite my gentle sucking he continued to get soft. He told me I was beautiful. He told me I had a great body and that he loved the sex. He said he'd never had his balls licked before or had his cock sucked after sex, but he still didn't get aroused again. When he started speaking about the cardiology talk earlier that evening, I knew it was all over. I went back to my room and masturbated, which is like being on a teeter totter by yourself," I summarized and then continued speaking about the next day.

"He was even more attentive and eager the next day at the conference telling me how he wanted to pleasure me that evening. I was excited to think tonight might be my night and didn't want to waste any time making small talk over dinner so I suggested we have a drink in his room after the last session. As he was opening the wine, I kicked off my heels and pulled up my dress, showing him I hadn't worn panties. He sat across from me and moaned with pleasure so I stood up and removed all my clothes, sat back down and spread my legs. I was certain he was coming over to lick me when he put his wine glass down and stood up. He started to slowly remove his clothes instead. As he was unbuttoning his shirt, I lifted one of my legs, placing my foot on the chair and began rubbing my clitoris. He unzipped his pants and allowed his hard cock to pop out of the top of his underwear as he stared at my hand pleasuring myself.

"That looks fantastic!" he said. "I've never seen a woman do that to herself before."

I spread my legs farther apart, exposing more to him, continued to rub myself, wanting and inviting him to touch me. After removing his pants and socks, he walked over to where I was sitting, stood in front of me and started to pull on his cock. After a few minutes he took me by the hand and led me toward the bed. When he sat on the edge of the bed and placed his hand beneath his balls and began moving his hard cock I couldn't resist putting it in my mouth. He rubbed my back and reached beneath me to squeeze my nipples as he moaned with pleasure. I ran my tongue up and down the shaft of his penis and around the head of his cock while I gently cradled his balls. When I felt his breathing become more rapid and his cock start to swell, I swallowed his cock deeper in my throat until he shook with orgasm and filled my mouth with his cum. I swallowed and gently licked until he collapsed backward on the bed grasping my arms and bringing me up with him. When he pulled me on top of him I thought he might roll me over and return the favour, but he held me tight against him instead. Again he began telling me how mind blowing the sex had been for him and how beautiful I was. It was only a few moments later that he began to suggest we go out for a bite to eat. Food was the absolute last thing on my mind at that point. My craving for the taste of cum in my mouth had been pleasurable, but I needed much more than that.

I got up off the bed, dressed and left his room without saying another word. I wanted to scream at him and tell him "eat me asshole!" I was beside myself with desire. I'd exposed myself to him, pleasured him, and invited him to let go of his inhibitions by telling him to fuck me. All he did was pull on his own cock! I felt like walking into the lounge and yelling "*Who wants to fuck me? Anyone? Finger fuck? Lick me? Line up starts here!*" As I was walking down the hallway toward the lounge, a text came to my cell phone from the girls asking me to FaceTime. I ignored the message, I was on a mission, but when I got to the doorway, something overpowered my lust and stopped me from going in. I took the elevator back up to my room and called the girls. I could barely concentrate on the conversation and when I saw Ken pacing back and forth in the background, I knew I needed to be very aware of what I was doing and how I sounded. Seeing him simply added insult to injury and I collapsed on the bed after ending my conversation with the girls. Why the fuck did I think this would make things better. All I did was get some asshole off, twice.

*"It is out now, we will speak of this another All you need to know is you will be speaking of ( things to get them out. Do not hide this."*

I hated the thought of having to speak about all the things I had kept buried for so long. I had so many questions and wanted to understand more.

"*You are full of questions. The one that knows you told me this.*"

"The one that knows me? Who do you mean?" I enquired.

"*Your mother.*"

If I understood correctly, he was talking about my Mom.

"She's with you? My Mom?" I asked excitedly.

"*Yes.*"

"Does she know I'm here?"

"*Yes, she knows you're here. You have felt her. You know she's with you.*"

"I've felt her?!"

"*Yes. Remember when you were falling off the bridge? And when you were exercising? Who did you hear when you were falling? Who do you speak to when you need help?*"

"My Mom! She was with me. I knew it. I felt her. Years ago I was hiking on a mountain trail and the bridge over a rocky creek didn't have side railings. It was sloped and slippery and as I was crossing, I lost my footing and fell over the edge into the water eight feet below. When I was in the ⁀, I heard a voice reassuring me that everything going to be okay and I felt calm. I landed with both of my feet planted firmly in between rocks and logs in the water. It was a miracle. If I'd landed any other way I would have broken an ankle or worse. I knew it was her! I even told the friend I was hiking with that my Mom saved me. It was just like the time I was on my road bike. I was riding alongside traffic through construction where they were replacing a bridge and as we were coming through, a car forced me off the road. I had no place to go but down the bank toward the river. As I was headed down toward the water, looking for a way to save myself, I heard her telling me it was okay, I'd be fine. And I was. I cartwheeled head first and somehow managed to let the bike keep going while I landed on the bank. My bike disappeared in the water, but I was fine. I knew she'd been there again and I'd often asked her to help me during the nights when I was crying and desperate because of the problems between Ken and I.

*"You have questions my Powerful One?"* he enquired again and interrupted my thoughts.

My head was spinning thinking about my Mom. I had so many questions, but didn't even know what to ask first at that point. I was overwhelmed and a bit confused by the enormity of what was happening. I didn't know who either of them were at this time.

"Who are you? What did you mean when you said you had always loved me? What's an aerial?" I asked quietly.

"*You can call me Magnus. The aerial is where the voice is coming from. We've been together before and we use an aerial to speak each time,*" he explained and continued. "*I wish you to think about this. Have you ever relaxed enough on the first time with a penis to get on top and allow your juice to come out? And then run to find him the next day to get more?*"

"I needed more! Not to get sex. I just needed to be near what I felt. To be close to him. To be with you! This! Everything! I don't know. I just needed it! And no, I've never been able to touch myself and orgasm like that before. I don't understand why I was able to do that, but for the first time in my entire life it wasn't just about the sex!

"*That is because you have felt this before. It is a feeling you have had and is one you've been craving since childhood. We have been together before. You have felt this. That is why you have been searching and why being with another penis has never satisfied you. It is not because of them. It is because you can't get back to where you've been before.*"

"What do you mean? In another life? I don't understand." I was exasperated and confused, yet somehow relieved to hear him so easily translate my feelings and struggles.

*"Stay on your path my Powerful One. You will get everything you want."*

"Stay on my path?" I asked. This must mean I'll be back with my family I think.

*"I've used enough energy this day speaking to you. I must let the aerial out soon."*

"I don't understand. What do you mean energy?" I asked.

*"Enough questions. I will speak through the aerial now when I speak. He will not know what we're talking about. Tell him about your problems with the soulmate. Do you understand?"*

"Yes, I believe so. He won't know what I'm talking about now."

*"Correct. You may say anything. He will not hear. I will hear now. I cannot do this for long, but it will be more clear for you. Understand?"*

I nodded yes.

*"I can't hear nodding."*

"I mean yes. I understand."

# CHAPTER 3
## Accepting The Truth

We dressed and returned to the kitchen and I spent the next hour describing my situation to Tom as he listened in silence. I was embarrassed to say Ken and I had been sleeping in separate rooms in our home for the past six months unfortunately allowing the tension to escalate. We had very serious financial problems and despite my continual pleas for outside help Ken refused, saying a financial restructuring accountant had no idea about real estate or our situation. He absolutely refused marriage counselling, but did say I should seek counselling on my own if I felt it would help me.

When I finally had the nerve to speak confidentially to his parents one afternoon, they told me I was over reacting and should listen to what Ken was saying. In fact, they had just put their savings into buying a rental property with their neighbors, the Rudays, because they were assured by Ken and his associate they could double their money. They told me Ken was working with a very experienced realtor who's also focusing on this area now because the "gold rush is going to happen right here, but it won't be gold, it'll be a real estate boom". They said Ken had finally found his niche and they weren't the only ones to see that. If I were the kind of wife I should be, then I'd be supporting him like they were. His parents said he just listed a boutique commercial space with a rental unit above it that will carry itself. He told them if they bought it, he'd drop his commission to three percent and if they bought it in their daughter Katie's name, they would save on tax as well. Ken's thought of everything they said! I argued that my commercial property was supposed to carry itself too, but never has. There's no guarantee in real estate and it's a big gamble. His mother spoke up at that point saying the expenditures such as the electronic medical record system I'd just incorporated into the practice was the reason my commercial building wasn't paying for itself. That was ludicrous and I could hardly believe they would say such a thing. I'd owned the property almost ten years and have always had to cover the entire mortgage on the building because the rental unit hasn't consistently been occupied. My attempt to engage his parents only made things worse as the next morning Ken forced his way into the bedroom when I was dressing and started yelling at me because I had spoken to his parents without his prior approval. He raised his hand to me which made me cower in the corner. It was then that I noticed the girls had come into the room behind him. At that point I had to do something. I said I believed the separation would only be temporary, and my leaving would allow us time to cool down and re-evaluate without so much tension around. Our financial stress was ruining our marriage.

"*What do you want?*" Magnus's voice returned.

"I want to keep my family together. We need to get out of the financial mess we're in and we can't seem to agree on how to do that."

"*I will help you to put the words inside the soulmate. The words have been outside not inside. This is how we will change the thoughts of the soulmate my Powerful One.*"

"What do you mean?"

"*When you speak the words, they are outside and the emotions get in the way. When he reads the words, they go inside. No emotions. Listen carefully. The aerial will speak to you now. Do you understand?*"

"Yes, I understand."

With that, Tom started to speak. "Send an email to him explaining how you feel. The emotions are getting in the way and he doesn't hear what you're saying. This way, he will see the words and they will go in."

After we said our good nights and Tom had left, I recalled the last time Ken and I had tried to talk. Sending an email made sense to me.

"We need to unload property, Ken. Not just sell property, but fire sale it. We can't make our payments. We need to list everything, including our house so we have a better chance of doing that. We have no choice."

"I won't sell anything without making profit on it, Tesh. You're talking like a child, not like someone who knows real estate and property development because you don't. That just doesn't make sense. If we leverage, we can hold on for at least another nine months to a year. It's going to be uncomfortable, but that's exactly what we have to do. Why won't you listen to me? This is what I do. You haven't been involved up until now and suddenly you think you know what we should do! You've obviously lost all faith in me and I'm getting really tired of taking the blame for all of this. You chose not to be involved so don't think you can walk in and suddenly run the show."

"I'm not running the show, Ken. I'm being realistic. We need to think about our future and the kids. I love you. I don't care what we have or don't have, but this debt is killing us."

"I am thinking about the kids. I'm the one that's been trying to give us a future. I'm tired of your disapproval. My love has always been free flowing. Yours is based on taking out the garbage and doing my share of the housework. Nothing I do is good enough for you, Tesh."

That was our last conversation and I was still numb from the words and tone of voice of the man I'd spent the last twelve years with. It was unfair and untrue. I'd tried very hard to be supportive of what felt like more than we could handle. I tried to convince myself that he knew what he was doing and would never put his family at risk, but I became more nervous as time went on and eventually started to say it just didn't feel right. He'd tell me that unless I had something concrete besides what my gut told me, he wouldn't even listen to me. And when I became aware of how desperate our financial situation was, I never once said it was his fault.

The more I spoke up, the more he withdrew from me. I told him I loved him and when I tried to ask him why he wasn't interested in having sex he had various excuses. For a while it was that he was a "morning man" and now it was difficult because he was worried one of the girls would come into our room, even though we had a lock on the bedroom door. Then he said it was because he was thoroughly exhausted from building his business and just didn't think of sex. Truth was, it had been years since he had initiated sex. He was uninterested and it was only getting worse despite my efforts to get closer, be more supportive, do more to allow him to do less. Whatever, he seemed to be pulling farther and farther away. I remember watching television together one evening on the weekend; I was rubbing Ken's feet and wanted to have sex with him. He eventually pushed me away and said, "Tesh please I'm just trying to relax. It's been a really busy week and I'd just like to shut my brain off." Those words made me feel worthless.

I thought about the parties we'd hosted at our home. Ken told me he wanted to develop relationships with other realtors and prospective clients so we had many parties around our pool. Although they were exhausting for me, I wanted Ken to be successful. I was starting to realize now, however, that I also felt good about the way he treated me in front of other people. It was one of the rare times he would actually put his arm around me and it made me feel that I was part of something. Ken would buy steaks, chicken breasts and more expensive wines than usual, then expect me to make appetizers, salads and desserts. Rather than help to host the party, he would make his rounds talking to everyone while I stressed about feeding the masses. I was always grateful when the realtor husband of my patient Kathy would jump in to help me barbecue. Reg seemed to understand how I felt and even told me he was often in the same boat while his wife was "out there" promoting her business.

During one party, while I was getting more ice from the kitchen fridge, Tom's golf friend, Bob, came up behind me and put his hand on my bum, telling me I was "looking good tonight". I knew he'd had too much to drink so I made light of it, laughing and moving away knowing he'd regret his words tomorrow. As I left the kitchen, however, I heard him say he'd be there for me if I ever needed. At the time I just thought he was drunk. When a similar thing happened at our next party with one of the realtors from the office where Ken worked, I started to wonder why both had been so sexually forward with me. Nothing like this had ever happened before despite there having been many parties that involved drinking and dancing around the pool and hot tub. It was almost as if they knew I was starving for affection and I began wondering if I was giving off some sort of different vibe. With all of this, I started to hate the gatherings and they were very expensive, too. One night after a particularly long one, I asked Ken if he thought we should be having so many costly events. Rather than thank me for all the work I'd done that weekend or reassure me that the parties resulted in an increase in house listings and sales or even tell me he'd do all the clean-up in the morning, all he said as he sat with a glass of wine in his hand while I was picking up empties was, "This is exactly what we should be doing, Tesh!"

I missed our two daughters and was devastated to think what this would do to them. They were both so trusting and seemingly unaffected when we told them Mom and Dad needed to spend some time apart so we could work on some problems without fighting in front of them. They were looking forward to staying at the townhome, and Ken had reassured them they would have two of everything at each of our places. I knew I needed to give this one last try before giving up on my marriage.

By the next morning, I had composed a well thought out email.

*Dear Ken,*

*One of our best days together last summer was spent on our boat with the girls. I know you'll remember the day I'm referring to because we both commented afterward how relaxing and enjoyable it was. We anchored off shore at Big Point Bay to spend the afternoon swimming, watching other boaters, and enjoying ourselves doing absolutely nothing. It truly was a magical day for me, Ken, and I want you to know it had nothing to do with the boat or the toys that come with the boat. It had everything to do with being together as a family. I would have had just as much fun floating on blow up mattresses. I don't care about what we have or*

*don't have, Ken. I love you, the girls, and being together as a family. That's what matters to me.*
*Tesh*

I pushed send and closed my iPad. There came no reply that day or the next. What did happen, however, was a chance meeting of Ken and I on a residential street in our neighbourhood. We both pulled over and I walked toward his truck.

Ken spoke first.

"I got your email, Tesh. I needed to think about it some more before I replied." I nodded and waited as I often did when I was interviewing patients. It was a skill I'd learned early on and as with my patients, I was rewarded with more information.

"It was a really nice email, Tesh. Thank you. But I think what we need to do is work out our financial problems and then see if there's anything left for us to build a relationship on. If we can work through the financial stuff, then I think we just might be able to find our way back to being a family again. You've not put everything on the table, Tesh. I've put everything there already for us. If we use your business, the building I mean, and leverage it, we can hold out until something sells. I'm willing to put everything up for sale, but at a reasonable asking price. If you agree, then I will make an effort to bring our relationship back to where it should be."

"I see," I said wondering what he had brought to the table, his clothes and a well-used road bike? I turned and walked away. The email message hadn't seemed to make a difference for Ken, but I remember this conversation being the turning point for me. Ken's words had finally sunk in and I understood why Magnus had me do this. The email wasn't for Ken, he was never going to change, but I had to see it and live it to understand it. My car wasn't far, and as I walked down the street and crossed, I shed the last bit of hope for our relationship and let it fall away in the middle of Circle Drive. Hearing him say finances were more important than love was affirmation of a very broken foundation. There was nothing here to build a relationship upon. I would go bankrupt with a man that loved me, but would not fight for a marriage based only on money and possessions. I phoned and made another appointment with the lawyer.

The girls spent the next few days at the townhome with me. On those days, I drove to work, dropping them at school on my way and picking them up at their after-school program on my way home. Their room had bunk beds, a perfect way to introduce room sharing to two girls who had never had to share a thing in their lives. We ate pizza and watched movies in our pajamas on our last night together. It was a fun couple of days for them at the end of their school year which was to be followed by a visit to their grandparents for the next week. The girls told me their Dad was going away on a golf trip and then they'd be spending the weekend boating at his friend's cottage when he got back. I remember wondering which one of Ken's friends had a cottage, none that I knew of. They were so excited I didn't want to say anything that might spoil their enthusiasm so I didn't question them about the cottage or say anything more about the separation.

I'd made coffee with breakfast that week while the girls were there and hadn't been to *Witch Brew?* at all. I wondered if Tom would still be coming on the weekend as I had no way of contacting him. My appointment with the divorce lawyer was on Friday after work and it left me feeling exhausted. I went straight to bed when I got home that day, that kind of stuff made me feel sick so dinner was out of the question.

# CHAPTER 4
## Second Chances

The next morning I'd showered and was dressing when the doorbell rang. I opened it to find Tom standing with his two arms full of brown paper grocery bags.

"I'm here to make brunch. Heading to the kitchen. You know the place, it's where you keep all your take-out food boxes!" he sarcastically chirped as he kicked off his shoes.

I moved to the side allowing him to enter, thinking he must have noticed the take out boxes in the garbage when he was in the kitchen last weekend.

"Who else is with you and how many, you've enough food for an army," I commented as he lumbered past with his load.

"Your message said you hadn't had time to shop this morning so I thought I'd get a few extra things for your week ahead, too. You'll need food for lunches." My message I wondered? I hadn't sent a message, but thought better of saying anything.

He busily unpacked the bags, loading things into the fridge and cupboards, obviously at home in the kitchen. Within a few minutes, he had coffee prepared and was cooking bacon and eggs while I sat at the counter in awe. I couldn't believe how wonderful it was to have breakfast made for me.

"You must like to cook, Tom."

"Yes, I've always enjoyed cooking, especially for other people. The more people the better. I used to make breakfasts on Sunday mornings for the guys from work. There'd be ten or twelve people show up and I had fun doing it. I don't know why, I just always wanted to make food."

Tom talked about growing up in a large family on the east coast. This seemed to explain what I thought to be the hint of a Scottish accent, his impeccable manners, and why he was such a gentleman. I had a couple of "Newfies" in my practice who I liked particularly because they were gentlemen, and funny, too. Tom's father and mother worked hard raising their six kids and although they were poor, they didn't seem to lack in creativity or mischief making. Tom was the eldest of the kids and left home at the age of sixteen to earn his own way. He hadn't finished high school and started working in a local service station sweeping floors and pumping gas, a typical grease monkey as he referred to himself. You could tell by his broad shoulders and muscular arms he was a hard worker and I assumed productive as brunch was prepared within a very short time. I learned he eventually became a mechanic and owned his own businesses, too.

"How did you end up here on the west coast of the country then?" I enquired.

"Well that's something I've wondered many times actually," he laughed. "I never wanted to move here. When my buddies would talk about moving west for work, I remember thinking well I'd never move there for work or anything else, yet here I am."

After a few moments he continued. "I was with a woman for ten years when I was back east. It wasn't the best of relationships and there was no love between the two of us, but she had a boy that I cared a great deal for and like so many others, I ended up being there for the wrong reason. Josh wasn't my son, but I looked after him and made sure he had the proper upbringing. I knew if I left, he wouldn't have had the opportunities he did. He became a really good ball player and got a college scholarship in the U.S.. She eventually wanted to be closer to her family and I found myself moving out here with them. I don't know why really, it would have been the perfect time to leave at that point, but instead when Josh moved away to go to school a couple years later, I left shortly after. I still keep in touch with him of course, but I have no communication with her whatsoever. I just never moved back east. It's weird, I don't even like it here that much and I've been here 5 years now," he laughed.

"You don't like it here? Really? But you must have friends here now."

"Nope, not really. I just don't like being around a lot of people, or being in crowds. I can't handle it. People say too much when they're not talking."

"People say too much when they're not talking?" I slowly repeated. "What do you mean by that, Tom?"

"Want some more coffee?" he asked as he grabbed our plates and started to clean up and I repeated my question.

"What do you mean by people say too much when they're not talking, Tom?"

"I find people lie most of the time," he began.

"People lie most of the time?"

"Yes, people lie! Even you!"

"What do I lie about?" I asked, a bit exasperated.

"Well just look at Facebook for example. They post pictures of themselves, smiling and having fun with friends or of their beautiful families with captions saying how wonderful their lives are, how proud they are of their kids and then the next thing ya know, they're divorced and scraping the

Daddy stick figure off the family van window so it's just Mom, the kids, and the cat. And now Dad is an asshole because Tommy just got busted for smoking pot and it has to be Dad's fault somehow. It's all bullshit!"

"Yes, I guess that's true, we pretend to have perfect lives on the outside when we're dying on the inside, but I like keeping in touch with my friends on Facebook," I commented.

"Is it maybe because you don't actually want to take the time to talk or meet? It's easier to push a button telling them you like their photo, and then you post a picture and let others assume your life must be wonderful, too?" he enquired. "Living a lie is easier than facing the truth?"

"Yes, I think that might be true. It's easier to have a lot of friends that way," I laughed. "They don't take up so much time. It's sad but true. I guess it's easier to pretend everything is good when you don't actually have to hear yourself saying it out loud to someone else," I admitted as I held up my cup and cheered towards him.

"Social media has allowed all of society to become liars, Tesh. Bullies don't even have to be physically strong anymore. Their strength is in what they type, and in the numbers of others they gather with them. A bully may never even have to come face to face with the person they're bullying so it's easy for them to continue raging on. What people haven't figured out yet is that all they have to do is shut it off. Not engage in the social media, the lies, but for some reason they don't or can't. They'd rather take the abuse. They'd rather punish themselves."

"So you don't have friends because they lie on Facebook?" I queried again.

"No Tesh. It has nothing to do with Facebook, but I don't use social media although I do like online banking and email. It makes life easier. When I was growing up I hung out with my siblings or by myself. I had a few buddies growing up, but I always seemed to spend more time with their sisters."

"Oh! I seeeeee," I teased.

"No, it wasn't like that, but I knew that young girls needed to be talked to and no one takes the time to do that other than their Mothers, and even then it's usually about rules and what they should and shouldn't do as young women. I felt even the Mothers wanted someone to talk to, especially someone that would listen to what they had to say. There were various reasons I hung out by myself," he took a big drink of his coffee and then continued.

"I remember when I was about eighteen and a guy I worked with at the time was talking about how great he and his girlfriend were getting along. They were gonna get a house together, and everything was roses. But when he was speaking to me, what I heard was him wondering if she'd been cheating the night before with his buddy. That first experience was really weird for me, and a few days later, I found out they'd broken up because he caught her cheating with the friend. It was crazy, I didn't understand it at the time."

"So you read people's minds?" I asked.

"Not really. I feel what they're feeling or thinking. I know when people are lying because what's coming out of their mouth isn't what's in their head."

"Oh, wow! That's a gift!" I immediately wondered if he'd felt my thoughts about his body, particularly his shapely buttocks!

"It's hard when I'm in crowds or at a house party. I can't control all the thoughts and feelings coming into my head. I've learned how to manage it, but I can't stop it."

A few moments of silence passed and I excused myself to use the washroom while he finished packing the dishwasher. He was putting his shoes on when I came out.

"We should get going to the flea market or we'll miss all the good deals," he smiled mischievously, turning to leave as I grabbed my flip flops.

"And thank you for noticing," he pretended to be embarrassed, wiggling his backside as he stepped out the door. I stood up to follow, feeling embarrassed and with a quick jolt thought about what Magnus had said about hiding my thoughts from Tom. He will see what I hide.

The drive to the flea market was like going to the fair as a kid. I was excited to be doing something fun and relaxing and Tom certainly kept things that way with his quick wit and sarcastic sense of humour.

"Tesh, I never make fun of people in public you know. Actually I don't make fun at all, I just point things out that are, well, you know interesting or obvious."

"Oh I know that, Tom. I would never think that you made fun of anyone. Nor would I ever do that either."

"Woah, now would ya look at that, she's got two bums, one out front and one behind," he said as we drove past a very large woman. "I hope that's a diet slushie she's drinking."

We walked from booth to booth, picking through the items for sale and commenting on everything and everybody interesting and unique. Tom had a very good eye for antiques, especially jewelry and glass, and talked about the value of different pieces from different eras. I was having a wonderful time. After an hour or so of walking, I needed to pee so Tom suggested having a "pint" on one of the outdoor patios on the main street of downtown Colmer. When I came out, Tom had ordered a couple of pints and was sitting with a bird's eye view of the passersby. He gave the salt shaker a shake into each of our beer and held his up to cheer.

"It's okay Doc, salt won't kill ya. Continually missing dinners like you did last night might though."

Caught again I thought as I realized that Tom's voice had changed slightly. He reached into the front pocket of his jeans and put his closed hand toward me across the table.

"This is for you," he said and turned his hand over to reveal an antique pendant, but unlike any I had ever seen. The main body looked like a very tiny flask, rectangular in shape and decorated with raised designs of fans, flowers and crescent moons with a fringe of six short chains hanging beneath the flask that jingled when it moved. It had a lid on the top that was attached to a small piece of chain. The entire pendant was silver, but blackened in areas indicating its age, and was attached at either end to a long silver chain. When I put it on, the pendant hung at my belly button.

"It's beautiful!" I gasped trying to think of when he might have bought it that day.

"You're beautiful. That's just a necklace. It will become part of you now. Each day you will dip it in your wetness. Open the lid."

"This is you speaking Magnus?"

"*Yes.*"

I opened the lid to reveal it had a one inch silver stem attached to it.

"You want me to put this part inside my vagina each day?" I asked sheepishly, holding up the lid with the stem on it.

"*Yes, every day. This is now the responsibility of you to take care of it. No one touches this but you or the aerial.*"

"May I ask why? What is this for?"

"*This connects us. If it is gone, we are gone.*"

"I don't understand," I stammered. "Please explain this to me."

*"What you need to know is this. If you want the connection, then you must do as you are told with the gift. If you do not wish it, then return it to the table. It is time you become the Powerful One."*

I liked hearing those words and wanted very much to be connected to something. I sat silent for a moment digesting the words he had spoken. With everything that was happening and despite my confusion about certain details, one thing was clear; the gift was not going back on the table. Tom's sarcastic voice broke the silence.

"That's her real hair colour!"

I started to take a sip of beer, turning slightly to see what Tom was referring to and almost spit my beer onto myself after seeing the young woman with a green Mohawk walking along the sidewalk.

"Does that remind you of when you were a kid and someone made you laugh at the dinner table and you had to go to your room after you shot your milk out through your nose?" he asked. Then a bit of it did squirt out onto the table as I tried to contain myself. I grasped the pendant that hung around my neck and tucked it inside my shirt.

"You don't need to hide it, just be aware."

As I looked at Tom and thought about these words, a drop of blood started from his nostril.

"Oh Tom, you're bleeding," I said and passed him one of the napkins from the table. "Do you get nosebleeds often?"

"Haven't had one for a while," he replied as he dabbed his nose. "I used to get them a lot."

After another hour or so of people watching slash bashing we made our way back to Tom's truck and then to the town-house.

"I had a great time, Tom. Thank you."

"I enjoyed it too other than you making fun of everybody all day, Tesh."

I laughed as I closed the door and walked around the front of his truck to cross the street. He waited until I was at the front door before rolling down his window.

"I'll make dinner here for you tomorrow night if you'd like, 6pm?"

"I'd like that very much," I replied and waved as he drove away.

I spent Sunday getting organized in the town-house, smiling, sometimes laughing and at one point crying as I compared the last week to my twelve years of marriage. I realized I had actually started to believe that love was what we had, where we lived, and what we wanted people to believe about us rather than what we felt between us. I was trying so hard to believe what Ken's vision for us was that I'd lost sight of what my own beliefs about love were. I was no better than him. Love wasn't something you found at the jewellery store, the country club or a beach in Hawaii. What I have just felt this past week is what matters and it can't be purchased. It's priceless. I realized I had just spent one of the best days of my life with someone at a flea market spitting beer onto myself because he made me laugh. The only thing I regret about this past week was telling Tom I only ever wanted to be his friend, and him confirming that all he wanted was a friend.

As I unpacked the last few boxes, I thought more about my relationship with Magnus and Tom. I've always considered myself to be intuitive, open to the possibility of communication between our reality and one that is somewhere beyond, not necessarily palpable, but real. This despite my scientific education, factual and evidence based. And Magnus had already confirmed that when he said my Mom was with me. I've also believed life is a balance of what we have sound evidence to prove for certain and everything else, including our gut feelings. Throughout my career, I've used my scientific knowledge and experience to make assessments and decisions while never letting it over-ride the thoughts, feelings, beliefs and experiences of my patients or even my own knowing. In science, there's something we refer to as the placebo effect, which means that when someone believes they're receiving treatment, they will experience improvement. Not only is our mind a powerful tool, our bodies and our existence is a combination of scientific fact mixed in with many, many unknowns. It would be arrogant to think otherwise.

I remember some of my experiences through my career. When a Mother of four insisted there was something wrong with her newborn baby, I listened. I remember reassuring her in those early days that everything seemed to be normal, but she insisted, pleading with me to keep looking, and I did. It turned out her infant baby had Cystic Fibrosis. It stunned the medical community that she was that connected to her newborn. I remember an elderly man who told me he did not want to go on living. His family was pushing him to move to a senior's oriented development because they felt he was too isolated in the house now that his wife was gone. They'd been married fifty years; she died of cancer a year earlier.

"I promised her I'd fill the hummingbird feeders. Once you start feeding them they come back to the same feeder the next year. I promised her. I can't leave her and the house where we raised our family. All our memories are there."

"What do you mean you can't leave her?"

"I make tea and we do the crossword together. She doesn't speak to me, but I know she's there. I can feel her around me. Inside I can hear her laughing and talking. It's wonderful. I'm able to get through each day knowing I'll be with her each evening."

I told his family it didn't matter whether they believed him or not, it was his wish to remain where he was. Fortunately they listened and he died at home in his sleep within a few months. Keeping an open mind as a physician has served me well. Medicine is not black and white nor is life.

It wasn't unusual for me to explore what I was experiencing, and I searched for information on the internet. I knew I needed to know more about what was going on. I spent hours visiting websites, everything from scientific medical organizations to spiritual channellers and psychics. I read information from the sublime to the ridiculous, and in the end I was no further ahead in terms of solid answers, but one thing I learned was there were a lot of people out there that claim to hear voices. I knew what I was experiencing was real, so maybe they are hearing something too. I would have liked to speak to somebody, but as many of us in the medical profession know, mental health or lack thereof is a reason for them to either jack up our insurance premiums or deny us altogether. After some of my research and my experience, I thought I'd better not say a word or I might just find myself holding a one way ticket to the cuckoo house. Besides that, many of the so-called experts looked a bit off their nut as did the religious fanatics so I chose to keep it all to myself for now anyway.

I had always questioned religion and even refused to go to church as a young girl. Punishing or killing in the name of one that was supposed to be loving and protective of the flock was confusing to me. How is it that God would choose to flood the entire earth because of a few sinners? Why not just punish the sinners? Then he would stand by and allow man to commit atrocities against one another for thousands of years without any intervention on his part? It just didn't make sense then and it still doesn't to me now. On the internet, I watched a video of a televangelist telling his viewers that if they listened very hard, they would eventually hear God's voice speaking to them. They would be able to tell if it was God's voice because "He will tell you to get up off the couch right now, kneel down, pray for God's forgiveness for your sins and He will open the gates of heaven for you!" This was quickly followed by information on how to send money to the show for "God's work". I laughed out loud at the absurdity of it.

"You'll know it's God's voice because he will tell you to give your money to the church. However, if the voice you hear in your head isn't telling you where to send your money, then you just might be psychotic!" I preached out loud, closing my iPad and standing up to stretch my neck and arms after a morning of staring at the small screen.

There was something fascinating about Tom and his ability to know of people's thoughts and feelings. I wanted to ask if he heard voices speaking to him or if he would describe it as something else. I reminded myself that I must be very careful asking this type of question to Tom. How was it that he didn't know about Magnus? How could that be? How could Magnus take over his body and mind without Tom knowing anything. It was unbelievable and yet more real than anything I'd ever heard of or experienced like this before. We all talk about our own intuition or knowing, and tell ourselves that our dreams mean something when they're vivid or colourful. We ask for a sign when we're perplexed or desperate, pay people to tell us our fortune, to read our aura, tarot cards, palms, and minds. We believe there's some truth in what someone spiritual tells us and yet I find myself questioning the validity of something that has literally overwhelmed me with how real it is!

I wondered again how is it that I should be this fortunate to be communicating with a spirit, an energy, and I was emotional thinking I might be able to speak with my Mom again. This thought made me smile, made me feel like crying, and made me believe that whatever was happening, it was good. Very good!

At six pm sharp, the doorbell rang and I raced down the hallway stopping briefly to gain my composure before opening the door for Tom.

"Let me guess, shopping today?" I teased as he handed me one of the heavy shopping bags.

"You don't have to worry; they're not hot like your grocery bags. I have to cook this first."

"Ha, ha, ha. I do cook ya' know!"

"Riiighhht."

Tom barbecued thick pork chops with baked potatoes and a simple salad of fresh tomatoes, avocados and cucumbers, while I sat and watched him move expertly around the kitchen. His cooking smelled wonderful and tasted delicious. Conversation had become so easy, it was refreshing to joke and I liked Tom's sense of humour. He was witty and made fun of himself. He made fun of me. He made fun of people from *Witch Brew?* and I laughed at the detail with which he noticed everyone's idiosyncrasies, accents and mannerisms. When he served dinner, he mimicked the very feminine mannerisms of the young man that served us coffee in the morning.

"Oh I love that colour on you Dr. Peterson! It brings out your eyes. I wish I could wear periwinkle blue!" he gestured with his hands on his hips, lisping and pointing with a broken wrist movement.

When his cell phone rang, I couldn't help noting he was speaking with a woman.

"Yes, Susan. That's fine. I'll see you at 2pm then," Tom replied and then hung up. He continued our conversation as if nothing was different. I couldn't help but wonder who he'd been talking to and for the first time in my life felt what I thought was jealousy.

We talked about business and managing people. I found myself sharing more about the business than I had ever shared with Ken. It occurred to me that I had never wanted my husband to have anything to do with my practice, but I was eager and open with Tom. I asked his opinion about many aspects of running the practice and he answered objectively and thoughtfully. It was wonderful.

"You mentioned you were semi-retired, Tom. What does that mean exactly? We've talked so much about me."

"Yes, I sold my last shop just before moving here. I dabble in a few things just to keep me busy," Tom replied, but still didn't explain the phone call I had overheard. I continued to wonder.

He cleaned up the dinner dishes and then we sat on the comfortable love seat in the living room. There were times when I wasn't exactly certain if I was speaking to Tom or Magnus, yet I knew Magnus was in charge of much of the conversation.

"*You're more relaxed now with the aerial?*"

"Yes I feel good, happy. He's funny and easy to talk to."

"*I will relax him in the bed. Come soon,*" and with that he walked into my bedroom.

We lay naked together in the bed as we had each time before. He told me it was my job to remember to stimulate the penis as this is what allows us to communicate. It was easier on the aerial this way he said. I found myself feeling strange talking about Tom as an aerial. He was my friend, and I wanted to understand more to be sure I was respecting him.

"*This aerial is different.*"

"What do you mean? His knowing what people are thinking, feeling?"

"*He can do more. You will see.*"

When you gave me the gift, you sounded like Tom. Why don't you do this all the time?

"*We can do this for a short time. It is hard on him.*"

"Yes, the nosebleed," I suddenly realized. "Has he always been an aerial?"

"*Yes, but we've been waiting to be with you.*"

"You were waiting to be with me first?"

"*Do you remember him speaking he didn't know why he came to live here?*"

"Yes I do. He seemed almost confused about why he wound up here. He doesn't even really like it here."

"*We needed him to come here, where you were coming. Think about yourself for a moment and why you came here. Does it make sense that you would move to this village?*" he asked.

"No it doesn't! It wasn't my idea to come here and I've often wondered why I agreed because it just didn't make sense for me to start a practice here. They have too many family physicians here already. It's been difficult for me to build up the type of practice I've wanted. And I'm the one that supported our family!"

"*That is correct. It has never been about you with your soulmate. We could not change the thoughts of the soulmate and you see this now.*"

I waited for a few moments and digested the words before speaking again.

"So you've been planning for us to meet?"

"*No. It was going to happen. It is your path. We tried to reach you when you were a child, but the one we were using did not work. He was too old and you were too young. The difference was too big. We could not do what we needed to do."*

"What do you mean? I've never heard voices like this before!"

*"You are too young my Powerful One. We will speak of this again."*

I tried to comprehend what was being said to me. It wasn't all making sense, but I didn't want to keep asking questions and have Magnus use too much energy to answer. Whatever that meant. I didn't want to harm Tom in any way. After a few moments, he spoke again.

*"Do you remember the first time you were with the friend of your brother?"*

This gave me a sinking feeling in my stomach and I felt shame and embarrassment as he asked me about my first sexual encounter, with Ben Douglas.

"Yes. It was my first time, with my brother's friend," I began.

*"Tell me about this time and pay attention."*

And with that I began to recall the day Ben waved at me to come in toward the barn as I was riding by. In truth, I had been riding past every couple of days after he'd suggested we could go for a ride together when we were swimming. Today he stepped out of the barn at the right time, and I was elated to think a fifteen year old boy actually wanted to ride with me. I tried to hide my enthusiasm by riding my horse slowly toward the barn, stopping at the trough to give him a drink.

"Hey Tessy! Let's tie Jack up inside and I'll get Blaze saddled up," Ben suggested as he motioned for me to dismount.

"Sure," I replied and dropped the reins before sliding off. Ben led Jack inside the cool, dark barn to the end of the stalls where he tied him up and gave him some hay. When Ben suggested I help him gather the tack for Blaze from the old wood shed I was thrilled. Johnny had often described the wood shed as their clubhouse and I'd wondered what it was like inside. I eagerly followed him out the back of the barn and into the small outbuilding known as the wood shed. It had a small couch and a couple of wooden chairs, posters of girls on the walls and a variety of things belonging to the boys including a football, baseball bat, and hockey sticks. As I was looking around, Ben grabbed me by the shoulders, started kissing me on the lips and then pushed his tongue into my mouth when he felt me start to relax. I'd never been kissed before and remember thinking it felt vastly different from what I had imagined or seen on TV. He was pressing so hard against me in the beginning that it hurt my lips, but he seemed to let up when he realized I wasn't fighting against him.

Ben pushed me toward the small couch and when I sat down, he forced himself onto me and I had to lay back. He kept kissing me and his hands moved over my body and then down to my pants. I didn't protest when his fingers went to my blue jean button and zipper as I felt a mixture of excitement and fear building inside me. He stood up and pulled off one of my boots and freed my leg from the blue jeans. He quickly took his pants and underwear down to his knees, exposing an already firm dink with hair around it. I'd only ever seen a dink before the day I had caught the boys play fighting at the swimming hole. He got on top of me, spreading my legs with his body and I could feel his hard dink pressing against me. He pulled my panties to one side and tried to penetrate me, eventually holding his dink with one hand and forcing it into me. I felt pain as he shoved it in. After a few pumps, he stopped moving and a pained expression came over his face. Within what seemed like seconds, he was standing up again, pulling up his jeans and doing up his buckle.

"Don't you tell anyone, Tessy. You come back tomorrow afternoon at three and I'll be done my chores then. Let's go," and with that, he left the wood shed.

I pulled up my jeans and put my boot back on, then returned to the barn where Jack was waiting. I felt pain between my legs as I walked to the barn and wondered if the wet feeling was visible on the outside of my pants. I led Jack out of the barn, quickly mounted and left the yard without looking around to see if anyone was there.

As I rode home, the pain between my legs kept me very aware of what had just happened. I fought back tears in fear that someone would notice I was upset and they might find out what I'd just done. I rode straight to the barn hoping no one would notice my arrival. After tending to Jack, I went to the house and quietly upstairs to my room without stopping by the kitchen as I normally might. Johnny was at my door within minutes.

"Tessy! Where have you been? It's hot, I wanted to go for a swim before dinner. Let's go!"

"Not today. I'm tired. I've been riding. I'm gonna get cleaned up for dinner now."

"What's the matter?"

"Nothing! I just don't wanna go. Leave me alone!"

I took off my jeans and panties noticing they were soaked with a mixture of a little bit of blood and a lot of sticky fluid. I put them at the bottom of my garbage can so I could get rid of them later. I wondered if this was what they called fucking. Is that all there is to it? Am I Ben's girlfriend now? Does this mean he likes me? He must have liked what we did because he wants me to come back again. It didn't feel that good to me, but I'm sure I'll get used to it I thought.

I'm not sure anyone noticed I was rather quiet at dinner that day, but the more I thought about what had happened, the more grown up I felt and by the next afternoon I was riding my horse as if nothing unusual had happened. The only difference was, I had somewhere to be at 3pm.

I described the experience to Magnus, continuing to answer his questions as openly and honestly as I could remember or be with myself. After all, if he knew about this one, he must know about all of them. His replies were never judgmental, and at times he would comment, "*remember this*", telling me to keep a thought or something I'd realized about the experience because we would be "*speaking of this time again*".

"Why do you want to know about this, Magnus?" I asked.

"*I don't want to know this. I already know all of your past. It is you that needs to know your past.*"

He hesitated and then continued, "*I need to speak through the aerial to explain this. Pay attention.*" Then Tom's voice continued.

"When you were young, even before reaching puberty, you were very curious about boys. You knew you were not like the other young girls. When you would be invited to their place to play with dolls you were more interested in what their brothers were doing. If the boys were outside, you wanted to be outside. You wanted to be near them, not playing with dolls. The only problem was you wanted to be around the boys that were not nice. This first one took advantage of you, and the next one and every one of them after that. You wanted the sex, you wanted love, but you didn't get either from them. They got what they wanted from you, including the Poison One. He got everything from you. Every one that came near you except for one we sent to teach you got what they wanted and all that you got was shame in speaking to us about these experiences. No one will ever take advantage of you again. I will not allow it. We will speak more about this. All you need to know and do now is stay on your path."

Stay on my path? What one had he sent? I didn't know what that meant, or exactly what my path was at that point, but knowing he was there to protect me was a wonderful feeling. I also had to admit that I did feel some relief after speaking to

Magnus about my sexual experience despite the embarrassment. I had often wondered if there was something wrong with me as a young girl. My fascination with sex and my inability to say no to anyone was very disturbing to me now as an adult. I guess I did need to understand my past so I could move forward and live up to my name, Powerful One.

"When you say Poison One are you referring to Ken?"

"*Yes.*"

I liked that name even more than the one he had given me.

"So did you also help the woman that the aerial moved here with. Was she like me? Did she know about the path?"

"*Yes. She was like you, and we tried for a very long time to get her to do the same thing. She could not stay on her path and that is why he is no longer with her.*"

I suddenly felt a bit of panic that I didn't know what he meant by "stay on your path". How could I do something that I don't even know what it is I need to do!

"*She was exactly like you with sex. From a very young age she willingly had sex with penises her age, older penises and penises the age of her father. She liked the older penises because they could be generous to her*".

"I had sex with young boys, but the older ones took it from me. I didn't go after it with them."

*"No you didn't go after it, but it was the path you were on at the time as she was also."*

"What do you mean they were generous?"

*"The older ones didn't make offerings to you. They just gave to you and you gave back to them. When they offered to her, she took and gave nothing in return. This changed her path from yours."*

What offerings? What fucking path was he talking about? How could I possibly understand what this meant? The only path I was seeing at that moment was one to a padded room! I wanted to understand so badly. This was a surreal moment and one that was beyond my ability to comprehend.

"Will you help me stay on my path? I don't want to make any mistakes, but I don't have much of an idea of what you're saying." I pleaded. Despite my years of education, I felt as confused and exasperated as a caveman trying to start a fire.

*"Do not worry my Powerful One. You will understand more with time and we will speak more of this soon. We need you to get there but this takes time. We will get dressed now and I will let the aerial out."*

"I want to know more now, please! Tell me more about her."

*"What was just spoken?"* he spoke sharply and I stopped arguing immediately, feeling for the first time the strength of the energy in his voice.

Once back in the living room, Tom's normal, funny demeanour was a relief from the twilight zone conversation I'd just had with Magnus. During those early days, Tom's unwavering friendship and support was at times the only thing that kept me upright and out of the sample cupboard in my office. Knowing my relationship with Ken was over was one thing, but coming to terms with the fact he seemed to want to take everything he could from me including my relationship with our daughters was cruel beyond belief. The girls were taken with Sandy who showered them with gifts and praised them at every opportunity. Soon they were telling me how happy Daddy was and how one day they'd both be flower girls at Daddy and Sandy's wedding. The legal process was exhausting both emotionally and financially. We eventually sold our home which cleared the house mortgage, but not before I was forced to sell the commercial building at a loss, leaving significant business debt and me with having to rent space from the new owners for my practice. I struggled to make ends meet and pay Ken support while he appeared unaffected, maintaining his golf membership and boating on weekends.

Tom often stopped by my office during lunch, bringing a still warm grilled sandwich, veggies and dip and sometimes a treat, often with a note warning me to eat the healthy food first or it would be the last of the treats. I remember late one afternoon arriving home after a particularly busy day with the girls and finding a roast chicken in the oven. My mornings would start with a phone call asking if I'd had a good evening and a reminder that it was recycling or garbage day, or to eat something before leaving for work. My favourite calls were the ones where he'd tell me he was coming over to make dinner that evening or would be delivering lunch to the office. Magnus would come out during our morning conversations to tell me he loved me and I naturally assumed the phone calls, at least, were his doing. Within a short period of time, Tom and I spent every evening together when the girls were with their Dad. I spent time with Magnus then as well and eventually could no longer contain my feelings for Tom.

"Magnus, I know I'm only supposed to be friends with the aerial, but I don't think I can do that any longer."

"*What do you mean?*"

"When you have him phone me every morning, I look forward to hearing your voice very much, but I also want to speak with Tom, the aerial I mean."

"*I'm not doing this.*"

"You're not having him call me in the mornings? What about bringing me lunch and spending evenings with me?"

"*This is your aerial doing these things.*"

"I think I'm falling in love with him. No, I know I'm falling in love with him, Magnus. I'm sorry."

"*I know this. Why are you sorry?*"

"I thought I was only to be friends with him."

"*Yes, friends first, until you make that decision. You are to be with the aerial. He is your aerial and will always be with you as long as you stay on your path.*"

I arrived home from work the next day to find Tom standing on the patio with a cold beer and a glass of wine set out on the table for us. I wanted to fall in his arms and tell him I loved him, but instead found myself fumbling for words and unable to say anything. He stood still, waiting, then gesturing with his face, smiling slightly as if encouraging me to spit it out. I eventually started to laugh and dropped my gaze, exasperated that I didn't know where to begin.

"You don't have to say it. I know what you're trying to get out."

"I wanted to ask how your day was?" I lied sheepishly and bowed my head further.

"*No*, that's not it." he replied softly, trying to make eye contact with me by moving his head down to meet my eyes as he spoke. "What if I said I love you, too, since the moment I first laid eyes on you."

I lifted my head up and met his eyes. "Why didn't you say something sooner?"

"I was having too much fun!" he said grinning mischievously. "I wanted to wait until you were ready, Baby. There is only one way to love and that's with true love. There is no need to rush."

When Tom and I embraced at last, and I repeatedly whispered "I love you" in his ear, Magnus spoke briefly.

"*You have the aerial's love. This is like nothing you have ever known. True love only gets stronger each day. Be prepared.*"

# CHAPTER 5
## Second Chances

Rex jumps off the love-seat as the phone starts to ring, jolting me back to reality. The house phone rings so rarely with its unfamiliar sound that when it does we pretend to be startled and excited by the unique occurrence. As I answer and hear a computer recorded voice, I quickly hang up, shaking my head and again wondering why we have landlines any longer.

I yell at Rex, "We just won another cruise to the Bahamas, all expenses paid except for the cruise, the food and all the booze. All we have to do is listen to a survey, but I got so excited I accidentally hung up. Damn telemarketers. Oh well, they'll call back next week I'm sure."

The light is starting to dim as evening approaches. I flick a switch as I walk into the kitchen and place my dirty dishes into the sink to join the ones from yesterday. If he doesn't get home soon, I'll have no plates to eat off. I smile and leave this unfamiliar territory thinking that I'd spent more time in the kitchen this week than I had in the last three years! Well maybe that's a bit of an exaggeration, but this is Tom's territory and we often joke that the only time I spend in the kitchen is to walk through it to get to the couch in the living room.

I'm restless without Tom at home. We've rarely spent a night apart in the past two and a half years since moving in together. And when we do, I get sick, not in the normal sense of the word, but more of a feeling of anxiousness, being unsettled and after two or three nights, a headache and upset stomach generally follow. It's easier if I'm the one at home, but I still feel the effects of our not being together. Tom teases me saying that it's probably just starvation or malnutrition, but it's real and I know he feels it too.

I remember the manila envelope of old photo in my bike pannier, and become excited to have the evening to sort through some of those memories. Rex follows me out to the garage, meowing in protest that I might be leaving again.

"Oh Rex, I'm not leaving. And if I were, you know I wouldn't forget to give you your cream first. If I didn't know better, I might think your love is based solely on who feeds you cream and treats, Rexxy Girl!"

I place the envelope on the floor and start to pick through the photos, laying them out on the coffee table as I look at them. I hold individual photos up, showing Rex what I looked like during those days.

"Look Rex, that's me when I was a baby. Yes it is. What a chunky monkey!" I describe. Rex seemed less than interested, not making the connection or getting the humour. Once she finishes licking her front left paw and washing her face, she stands and walks off toward her nest in the bedroom closet.

I call out to her, "Wait, here's one when I was older. You might recognize me in this one, Rex. Come back!" As I hold the photo up as if showing it to Rex, I realize that I hardly recognize myself. Or is it that I don't want to. As I stare at the photo, I remember what I was like those days.

A young woman standing beside a red Volkswagen, very short jean cut-offs and a swimsuit top, wavy blond hair in a ponytail and attitude written all over her face and stance. The only thing this one didn't have was a tramp stamp on her lower back, which I know my Mom would have never been able to keep me from doing at that point in her failing health, but I was never interested in tattoos. I didn't need the ink to define me, but that's pretty much what I was about then. Princes were hard to come by during my youth, but young farm boys were not. My desperate attempt to find love had led me to frequent visits to the Douglas wood shed the summer I turned thirteen. By the end of the summer I had started to enjoy the encounters, but then stopped going to the wood shed for some reason. I knew it had nothing to do with Ben's older brother Daren because I enjoyed that more than lying on my back while Ben pumped a couple of times for his relief. I recalled the first day with Daren, riding into the yard excitedly expecting Ben to come out of the barn as he usually did mid-afternoon, but being surprised to see Daren come out to greet me that day instead.

"Ben's not here, Tessy." Daren informed me as he walked up to Jack. The look on his face told me Ben had not kept his mouth shut as I had. He gave Jack a pat on his neck, held the bit with his other hand and gently pulled the reins from my hands.

"I'll take him inside now."

"Oh that's okay. I should get going anyway," I stammered. "Just tell Ben I stopped by."

"No Tessy. Get off. I've got something to show you in the wood shed."

As I dismounted, Daren turned and led Jack into the barn, tying him up as Ben had been doing for the last couple of weeks. I followed him out to the wood shed without speaking, but wondered what exactly Ben had told his brother about me. Once we were inside, he turned toward me, unbuckled his belt and started to undo his jeans. He motioned for me to come closer and when I did, he put his hands on my shoulders and pushed me to my knees in front of him. He finished unzipping his pants and pulled out his dink. It looked the same as Ben's but I'd never been quite this close before. When Daren put his hand on the back of my head, I then understood, with some shock, that he wanted me to put it in my mouth. I didn't know what to do with it in my mouth, but he started to move my head back and forth by gently pulling my hair and telling me to suck his cock. As he became more excited, he pushed his cock in deeper which made me gag a couple of times. Then it seemed to get even harder and he squirted in my mouth. I didn't know what to do with him holding my head and his cock in my mouth so I swallowed. I looked up at him from my knees to see the same look of pain on his face that Ben would get. What I didn't know then was that it was pleasurable for him, not painful. When he let my head go, I slowly pulled back and he tucked his cock back into his jeans. As he zipped and buckled himself, he started to speak.

"Ben isn't here on Wednesdays. He's working for old man Brown now for the rest of the summer. I'll be doing his chores those days so see you next Wednesday."

I nodded in agreement and he turned and left the wood shed. I stayed on my knees for another moment, the taste of what he put in my mouth made me feel like I wanted to spit, but I'd already swallowed it all and my mouth was dry. This must be what Ben puts inside me I thought. I stood and walked out the open door toward the barn, turning back to see what I believed to be Daren's shadow going around the corner of the wood shed, but a few minutes later when I was walking Jack through the barn I saw Daren going into their house ahead of me. That's strange I thought, but quickly forgot about it as my focus turned to what had just taken place inside the wood shed. I've never had a boyfriend before and now I have two I thought. I wondered why Daren wanted to put it in my mouth and not inside me like Ben had. Even though he hadn't put his cock inside me, I felt wet down there. This was all strange and new, but I was excited by the thought of another experience that made me feel older. As soon as I was back in my bedroom, I marked this day and every Wednesday for the rest of the summer with a tiny heart on my calendar.

I find it difficult to look at the photo of myself back then. At sixteen, I was confident in my sexual ability, I could fuck anything and knew how to make them cum quickly in my mouth so I could get to the next one, but for some reason I never went back to the Douglas wood shed after that first summer.

I shake my head and toss the photo back on the pile. I think of the bottle of red wine on the counter in the kitchen and decide a glass would make me feel more relaxed and able to continue my journey through the photos of my youth. I pour a generous amount into a stemless wine glass and return to my position on the living room floor. Another photo catches my eye and I lift it up to take a closer look. It's me during my graduation from University.

My marks in school had always been very good and I even won an athletic award during high school. For that I was grateful. So many of my friends had married right after high school and became farmer's wives, having babies in their early twenties. Although I wanted love, my relentless search had proven that Prince Charming was not in the small prairie community where I grew up

When I moved away to go to university, it was with the intention of becoming a doctor. I had to remain focused on my undergraduate courses so I would be accepted into medical school which didn't leave much time for satisfying my lust for sex. I did, however, manage to engage in several meaningless, empty encounters with university boys. I remember one particular Saturday morning waking up and heading to the main library. This library was a mixture of students from different programs and I enjoyed the variety and anonymity. I sat down a couple seats away from a guy who appeared to be fully engaged in his studies. He eventually looked up and we acknowledged one another.

"What are you taking?" he asked.

"Science mostly, pre-med. You?"

"BA. Planning on law. I'm Brett."

"Tesh. My friends call me Tessy."

We continued chatting and eventually he asked me to his room. His residence was close to the library and a typical guy's space, disorganized and stale smelling. We sat on his bed, talked for a few moments, and then started kissing. Our clothes came off shortly thereafter and soon we were fully engaged in some serious fondling and groping of one another's bodies. Then he rolled onto his side and reached into the top drawer of his night table, retrieving a vibrator. I remember thinking he must have had lots of girls over if he's got this kind of equipment for them. I'd never even seen a vibrator before although I'd heard about women having them to pleasure themselves. He showed me how to adjust the speed of the vibration and told me to touch myself where it felt good. I was a bit embarrassed, but soon found it to be quite enjoyable when it wasn't vibrating too quickly. He told me to hold it while he put his fingers inside me and within a couple of minutes I had my first ever orgasm.

"That was fantastic!" I exclaimed. And that's when I learned it wasn't meant just for me. He took the vibrator from me, pushed it inside me to get it wet and then slowly pushed it in his ass while he lay back on the bed pulling on his penis. I'd never seen anything like this before and became excited again as I watched his hand start to move faster on his penis, matching the increase in his breathing while he pushed the vibrator as far as he could up his asshole. As he became more and more excited, he stopped breathing and became red in the face, lifting his ass off the bed and stroking himself even faster. I placed my face and mouth close to his penis waiting for what I knew was about to happen and as he started to orgasm, he stopped the movement of his hand and I put my mouth on his penis and swallowed his cum. I kept my mouth there, moving it very gently and slowly, sucking and swallowing until he was soft. He lay motionless, twitching only when I touched the sensitive end of his penis, until I removed my mouth and collapsed on the bed beside him. We lay there for a few minutes in silence, allowing our bodies to recover from the adrenaline rush we'd just experienced. Before it became awkward, I stood up; picked up the pieces of clothing I'd tossed on the floor and dressed.

"Nice meeting you, Brett."

"Nice meeting you, too. Thanks."

"Same," and with that, I grabbed my backpack and headed back to the library. By closing the door behind me, I realized I had just opened another door ahead to a new sexual chapter. I'd finally experienced that pained expression! What excited me more, however, was realizing how much I enjoyed watching him masturbate and anticipating what his cum would taste like in my mouth. I craved this pleasure and this taste.

Later that semester I began to hang out with a couple of girls that were in several of the same classes as me. Their company helped me keep my thoughts on course work. It was different as I'd never really spent a lot of time with girls, and we had a lot of fun together, studying, working out and some partying, too. Laurie lived with her parents off campus and they let her throw a little party for a bunch of us girls after we finished finals. Her Dad, Roger, barbecued burgers and her Mom, Helen, served appetizers and salads. All those years on the farm with horses and I'd never played horseshoes. The evening progressed from outside to indoors, eventually everyone was drinking beer and playing cards. One by one the girls began dropping out of the card game, heading upstairs to change into sweats and finding a place to crash. I was one of the die-hard card players so was left to sleep on the pull out bed in the family room while one of the other girls slept on the couch in the same room.

Sometime in the night, I could feel the blanket being pulled up over my shoulders. I thought at first it must be Shawn, but as I opened my eyes, I could see the outline of her body on the couch on the other side of the room. Then I felt hands moving around my waist and up underneath my shirt touching me softly so as not to wake me. I rolled over onto my stomach and made some snoring sounds, hoping the person might think I was waking and would leave, but this predator was persistent, moving hands down the small of my back and then between my cheeks. The fingers moved down my crack and around my asshole. With a thumb pressing on my butt hole, I felt the fingers move in and then out of my vagina. I had become wet and although I wanted it to stop, I was enjoying the feeling of the fingers moving in and out and the thumb pushing on the outside of my ass. By now, whoever it was could have done anything they wanted to me and I would have pretended to be passed out, even if they had decided to fuck me. After a few more minutes of fondling, someone could be heard walking upstairs and the predator moved away from me. I turned my head when I heard footsteps moving toward the door to confirm what I already knew, that Roger, Laurie's dad, had been finger fucking me while I slept or while he thought I slept.

I lay awake feeling a mixture of shame and anger that my friend's dad would do that to me and that I had allowed it to happen. I could have pushed him away, but I didn't. I liked it! It felt wonderful and reminded me of the very first time I had been finger fucked by the scruffy old man in the van. While the memory of who was doing it to me makes me sick, I loved that feeling of fingers inside me.

The next morning the girls gradually made their way into the kitchen for a big breakfast made by Laurie's parents. I was careful not to let on that anything was wrong or that anything had happened during the night, but I couldn't help feeling disillusioned about love and relationships. I watched Helen standing beside her husband serving breakfast, smiling, laughing and lovingly putting her hand on his back when she spoke to him. He on the other hand was probably thinking about finger fucking me and who knows who else the night before. Seeing him act so naturally, as if nothing had happened, made me realize this was not the first time that fox had visited the hen house.

I looked so young in the university grad photo. I clearly remember the ceremony and my half-hearted attempt at celebration that weekend. For me, the work was about to begin as I'd already been accepted into medical school by the time that photo was taken. I then moved further away from home and was immersed in my second year of med school when my mom died unexpectedly. I'd seen her a couple of months earlier, but hadn't spoken to her for two weeks when she had a fatal heart attack. She wasn't well when I'd last seen her and it haunted me to this day to think I was a second year medical student and didn't see how sick she was. On the day I left, she was admitted to hospital with pneumonia and it was only then that I realized how pale and tired she was when I was visiting. I was so self-absorbed that I didn't see anything but myself. Losing her would prove to be one of the hardest things I would ever experience. Until three years ago, I believed there were no second chances, no opportunities to make things right or to be a good and loving daughter. Now, perhaps, I could have a second chance, even with my Mom.

If there was such a thing as a biggest fan, I believe that would best describe Mom. She spent hours sitting at the kitchen table with me while I worked on my homework during high school. I didn't spend a lot of time on math, the sciences or English, but my fascination with art often necessitated I spend several hours in the evening perfecting the outline of a woman's figure or working with different mediums such as water colour, charcoal or acrylic. Mom seemed to love watching this and although I was never going to be an artist, I'm now more grateful for those couple of years I spent trying to be one than all the knowledge gained through my years of medical school. I realized too late those times were the only ones that really meant anything at all during my youth and despite my taking them for granted, we had many laughs and meaningful conversations during my high school days. Although my Mom wasn't able to physically do what most other moms did with their kids, and at times that proved to be an embarrassment for the spoiled young princess that I was, I realize now this was a blessing because she was always there to sit and converse instead. When she was gone, her seat at the end of the table was never used again. It was as if it had been so imprinted with her presence that no one wanted to sit on her and hurt her after she was gone.

What I failed to realize during those high school years was how much the memories I shared with her meant to me. There were autumn evenings sitting at the kitchen table looking out over miles and miles of burning stubble in the grain fields. Many times Mom made picnic dinner to take out to Dad when he was finishing a project in the yard before leaving the next morning. She made many attempts to speak to me about being a woman and how I should be able to support myself so I would never have to rely on anyone other than me. Although I failed to see the meaning of what she meant, I did take off to school as soon as I graduated. I'm not sure that's what she meant, but leaving became more important than staying for me, and I guess I always expected she would be sitting waiting for me at the end of our kitchen table when I returned.

As I sit picking through the photos, I'm hit by the realization that Tom's teachings have been about the enjoyment of life, too. His stories about the good memories during his youth, being able to finally eat his length in corn and then he and his brothers eating double their length in corn to show how tall they were going to become. His continual humour about everything, simply everything, including my strong body odour at the end of a ride on my bike, my lack of interest in the kitchen and even more often his ability to laugh at himself. The fact that he wears wool socks winter and summer, and pulls them up as high as possible and walks around naked are memories that make me laugh just recalling those visuals.

I stop picking through the photos and decide to call it a night. I feel incredibly fortunate to have the second chances I'm having now, to heal the past and move forward into the future. I realize now there will be many opportunities for happiness ahead and the more that I deal with my past with Magnus and allow Tom's love to heal me, the more I understand what my path might just be.

# CHAPTER 6
## The Opportunist

Medical School was the best and the worst of times. I immersed myself in it, probably wanting to make up for what I hadn't been to my own family by giving myself to others. It was during Med School that I took up road riding as one of my main ways to keep fit, and I gave myself to it, too. Or should I say I gave myself to *"them"* as it was during this period in my life that I got to know *"The Three Amigos"* as I called them and opened up not only to road riding, but also to older men.

I had saved to buy a new road bike and was contemplating between two, having tested one and was about to take the other one out for a ride when three men walked into the shop to get chain lube before heading out on their regular afternoon ride. The oldest of the three, Steve, struck up a conversation with me about the bikes.

"Buying a new ride are you Missy?" he enquired enthusiastically. "Having trouble making a decision?"

"Yes, my budget while I'm in school says this one, but the rest of me says thiiissss one!" I say as I point to the more expensive of the two. "I'm afraid to take it out for a ride 'cause I think it might make it an even tougher decision in the end," I say.

"Why don't you join us. We're heading out for an easy flat one today. Maybe you'll like the other one better," Steve tells me as one of the other men walks up and seems to quickly catch on to the conversation.

"If you don't buy the higher priced one, you'll still have had a nice ride this afternoon with three distinguished gentlemen," he kidded. "More like three old geezers," he corrected himself, introducing himself as Lee.

"I'm Tesh. My friends call me Tessy," and I shake hands with him.

"Nice firm grip, stronger than Keith," he says as he sees his friend walking our way.

"He says that because I'm the youngest," Keith responds and holds out his hand. "Oh Ouch!" he says as he feigns being hurt by my handshake. "I've only been getting the special rates for a couple of years, unlike these two dinosaurs," he laughs.

I assume Keith is around 67 and Lee somewhere between there and 70 as I walk over to shake Steve's hand who I figured to be in his early seventies.

"I'm Tesh. Thank you. I'll join you for a ride then if you don't mind."

"And I'm Steve. That's a good girl now. Let's go!" he says as he stands and waits for me to lead the way.

The three of them start by keeping me in the middle of the pack so I can get comfortable with the bike without having to pull the group along. We ride at a very comfortable pace and once we get off the busiest streets and on to a quiet paved road outside of town, the joking starts again. Most of their humour is at their own expense, but the three of them seem to know each other well enough to continually tease, and very soon are including me in their fun.

"How's it up there?" Keith yells up to Lee who's leading at the time.

"I'm good here, but not as good as the old boy me thinks," he yells back.

"That's right! I'm enjoying the best ride back here. It's a wonderful view from the back. Lovely day," he yells up past me to the two others.

As we crest the top of a small incline and level out again, Lee moves to the back of the pack.

"Ah now. That's a good deal better indeed. I was finding it a bit tough up there actually. I think I might enjoy staying back here from now on," Lee comments.

It isn't until Keith moves to the back, allowing me to lead, that I finally catch on to their jokes about the view from behind being significantly better today and start laughing.

"I've been looking at their two old asses for years. So nice to have a beautiful young woman to follow behind," Steve kids as we pull off the road for a break. "I don't complain because it's still easier than pulling the group along, but I don't fancy either of them," he laughs.

"How's that bike Tesh?" Lee enquires.

"It's a cadillac compared to the other one unfortunately," I reply. "I know I'm having an easier ride being with the three of you, but it's over all a nicer feel for me on this bike."

The ride continues and we stop one more time before returning to the bike shop.

"I know the shop owner well, Tessy. Why don't I talk to him when we get back and see if he'll sweeten the deal," Steve quietly says to me before we start riding again. I tell him I doubt they can lower the price so it fits into my budget, but I thank him for offering to try. I'm surprised and delighted when he tells me later that he's managed to get the owner to sell it to me at the same price as the lesser one.

"He said he'd sell it to you at the same price, Tessy, but there's a hitch. You'll have to join the boys and I for a beer and then stay for dinner with me tonight."

"That's no hitch, Steve. You've saved me about $500.00!" I exclaim. "Thank you, I'll gladly join you and celebrate," I say as I clap my hands together at the thought of having a brand new bike to pick up tomorrow afternoon.

"Now that's a good girl. We'll meet you at 5pm at Brandy's Lounge at the Country Club on Mountain Way. Is that enough time for you to get cleaned up and over there?" Steve asks.

"Yes that's no problem. Is there a dress code there, I've never been?" I enquire trying not to look too excited to be going to an exclusive club.

"No, nice jeans are fine, Tessy. We'll see you there at five then. Your name will be on the guest list when you arrive at the front entrance. What's your last name?"

"Peterson. Tesh Peterson," I tell him and then head home to my apartment to get cleaned up.

An hour later I arrive at the club just before five. I've ridden past the main gates many times over the past year, admiring the beautiful grounds, but staying outside its boundaries as if it were a foreign country. Tonight I feel as though I'm crossing into a whole new world as I walk up the steps and into the foyer of the main building. The woman on the other side of the glass in the reception area greets me and asks if I'm with a member. My heart sinks as I realize I don't know any of their last names and I fumble for a few seconds before she becomes impatient and reframes her question.

"Are you on the guest list this evening?" she asks in a louder more nasal tone.

"Oh yes, I am!" I exclaim remembering Steve's instructions at last. "Tesh Peterson," I say with more authority now.

"Yes, Ms. Peterson. You're at Mr. Simmons table on the 19th," she replies with a sudden change in her demeanor. "Welcome, do come in," as she not only presses the buzzer to open the door, but jumps to her feet to greet me on the other side. "Allow me to walk you to your meet your party."

"Here she is!" Keith says, seeing me first and jumping to his feet as I walk toward the table of three men now all standing, which is next to one of the floor to ceiling windows, overlooking the golf course and an enormous fountain in the middle of a pond.

The waiter is immediately at our table and within moments has a glass of white wine in front of me. We raise our glasses in a cheer to celebrate my new bike and I'm surprised at how wonderful the wine tastes. I think it must be considerably more expensive than the ten dollar bottles of wine I generally buy.

"This is a beautiful view," I say as I look out onto the golf course. "What's the 19th?"

"That's the 18th hole out there and they refer to this as the 19th. This is the best hole on the course." Lee laughs. "We're fortunate enough to be able to sit at Steve's table which has this spectacular view."

"Now Tessy," Steve starts, changing the subject, "You said you were in school. I'm assuming that means university?"

"I'm just finishing first year Medical School," I reply proudly and notice how the three of them seem to be impressed as well.

"That's excellent!" Steve replies. "Will you be going into family practice or specializing in something?"

"I'm interested in general practice, but not closing any doors just yet. Like a parachute, I'm wide open, and if I don't look at it that way, I believe I'm gonna hit the ground hard. That's not what I signed up for." With that we all raise our glasses.

Our conversation continues, moving from my career plans back to road riding and then briefly to each of their lives before Keith and Lee both had to leave to join their spouses for their Saturday evening social plans. Lee was a CEO of a crown corporation and then a consultant in oil and gas before finally retiring a year ago. He and his wife have three grown children. Keith retired a year earlier after selling his successful accounting firm. He and his wife have two cats, no children. Steve appeared to be the wealthiest of the group, a widower with four grown children and two grandchildren. All four of his kids are involved in the management of his portfolio of companies and real estate holdings.

"Do you dislike any foods, Love?" Steve asks me when the waitress comes to our table with fresh drinks.

"I'm a student remember. I'll eat anything." I reply smiling.

"Good Girl!" he laughs and orders dinner for the two of us. The food was delicious and Steve seemed delighted that I ate every last bite. We spoke of our families and where each of us grew up. I said I'd always wished to have more siblings which made Steve laugh.

"I'd never give any of them away now, but I'm glad I got snipped when I did. Four kids was enough!" He laughs. After an hour or so, Steve signed the bill and ordered the valet to bring his car around. He wasn't surprised to hear I'd walked here from my apartment and insisted he drive me home saying it was too late for a beautiful young woman to walk home alone.

"I live at the end of Granite Avenue, on the way to the university hospital. Do you know where that is?"

"Yes, I know that area," he replied and started to drive.

"I can't thank you enough again, not only for the lovely evening, but also for speaking to the shop owner about the bike." I told Steve.

"Your lovely evenings don't have to end here, Tessy," Steve began. "Listen, at my age I'm not looking for a wife, someone to get their claws into me or my children's inheritance, but I would like to have occasional companionship," he explained.

I didn't reply immediately and was trying to understand exactly what he meant by companionship when he continued.

"I realize you're a very young lady and there's a big age gap between us. Mine is not the body of someone you might choose to be with, but I still have wants and needs. I'm very capable." He spoke as a businessman might and I appreciated his approach. I felt he was being honest and it made me feel like this just might be a good opportunity for both of us.

"You understand that I'm very busy in school and that is my priority. I do need exercise and breaks from my studies for other recreation though," I said as I looked at him and smiled.

"That's a good girl. Of course you do! We ride three times a week and sometimes more, generally around the same time as today. The boys and I keep our bikes at the club so we start and finish there. I'll give you my card when we get to your place so when you're not studying and want to go out for an evening, you can give me a call," he finished.

"It's Saturday night. I'm not studying now," I replied and without speaking he turned right at the next intersection. We drove for another ten minutes, arriving at a set of closed gates that opened automatically as he pulled up to them, reminding me of garage doors. The driveway was as long as the entrance to the country club and his home as palatial. I knew one thing for sure, he would have a staff of gardeners and cleaners for this spread! He parked in the garage and we entered through a side door into the main living area. Before all the lights were turned on in the house, I noticed a spectacular view of the city lights from the windows along the entire front of the home.

"It'll just take me a minute to get all the lights turned up and a bottle of wine for us," Steve spoke and I noticed an edge of nervousness to his voice which made me feel confident.

"Tell me where to get the glasses. We only need lights in here and the bedroom," I replied and walked into the kitchen area.

"Glasses are there," Steve pointed to a glass front cupboard as he reached into the wine rack and pulled out a bottle of red. I watched as he opened the bottle and poured into the two glasses, passing one to me and picking up the other.

"To a wonderful day," he raised his to cheer.

"And a lovely evening," I replied as Steve pointed toward the stairs in the next room.

"This way Sweetie."

I picked up the bottle and followed him up the stairs and down the hallway to the enormous master bedroom, setting my glass down on a small table in the sitting area just inside the door. I sat on one of the chairs and he sat across from me, crossing his legs and taking a sip of his wine.

"I'm glad you wore a dress tonight. You look lovely," he told me. It was a simple summer shift made of silky feeling multi-coloured material that loosely clung to the curves of my body. I liked how it felt next to my skin, but wished I didn't have to wear a bra with it. Generally I wore clothes that allowed me to go without a bra and if possible, without panties. Tonight, however, I wore both in white, thankful I'd recently purchased underwear that were more like boy shorts than a thong.

"Thank you," I replied, leaning back in the chair and lifting my feet up to the edge of the seat with a childlike motion, exposing my bottom beneath the dress.

"Oh that's so wonderful. What a lovely little girl you are," he spoke slowly and softly, shifting in his chair.

I stood up and took my dress off over my head, tossing it onto the back of another chair and standing in my bra and panties in front of him. I could tell he was mesmerized by my white underwear and had noticed how he continually referred to me as a good little girl. I liked how it made me feel and it was obviously exciting him as well.

"Will you take your clothes off for me, too?" I asked in a sweet, innocent tone as I removed my bra, and sat down on the chair again. He started with his button down shirt, and then took off his pants and underwear together. I was surprised but even more excited to see an enormous semi erect penis.

"Oh my, that's big," I said in the little girl voice and walked over to him, taking the penis in my hand and gently rubbing it. He in turn put his hands on my arms, gently moving them up and down as he looked down at my breasts. I could feel him shaking slightly as he touched me.

"What are you gonna do to me? I've never done anything like this before," I teased.

"Don't worry Sweetie, we'll just lie down together and relax." He took my hand and led me over to the bed, throwing the duvet aside and encouraging me to get in. As we lay facing one another on the bed, he started to caress my body from my head down to my buttocks on the outside of my panties.

"What a lovely little body you have. Does that feel good, Sweetie?" he asked as he rubbed my body, caressing my breasts with his open hands and gently squeezing my nipples between his fingers.

"Oh yes, that feels very nice. More please."

"Oh you like Daddy touching you there do you?" he whispered. It was at that moment I realized he wasn't just joking about me being a little girl. He was really into this.

"Yes Daddy. I like that very much. May I touch your big penis again please?" I begged, moving my hand down and grasping him again, noticing how much larger and firmer it had become since we'd moved to the bed and continued with our play. His hand slowly started to go beneath my panties and over my buttocks and into the crack of my ass. Then he gently pushed me with his hand and told me to lie on my back as he moved closer and started kissing my forehead, face and neck. As he caressed with his hand, he kissed and spoke.

"Daddy's little girl has such nice soft skin. Does that feel good?"

"Yes Daddy that tickles. You've never kissed me there before."

"That's a good girl," he continued to kiss, moving slowly down my belly to the top of my panties, and then pulling my panties down slightly and putting his face closer to my vagina. He kissed and inhaled through his nose as he explored my body. "My little girl smells so nice and sweet," he continued as he smelled my panties and then removed them, lifting them to his face and inhaling again. He spread my legs apart and moved in between them.

"Daddy wants to taste his little girl. Mmmmm," he moaned as he continued to smell and then gently started to lick. I was dripping wet by this time, surprised at how much I too was enjoying being his little girl.

"Daddy's gonna put his tongue in there now, Sweetie," he said as he slowly pushed his tongue inside my cunt. I moaned and raised my ass up slightly so he could push it in deeper. "That's a good little girl. You like it when Daddy does that don't you?"

"Yes, Yes, Yes, Daddy. More please more," I moaned and begged and not just for his pleasure. It was feeling really good. I squeezed my nipples as he gently plunged his tongue in and out of me. Then he pushed my shins toward my chest, raising my ass even higher off the bed and started to lick around my asshole.

"I like that too Daddy."

"You taste so wonderful my sweet little girl," he spoke as he licked and smelled between my legs. When his tongue finally went into my asshole I thought I was going to explode. It felt fantastic. He continued probing as I moaned and he spread my legs farther apart, eventually allowing my legs to come back down to the bed. I could tell he too was very excited and as he kneeled between my legs I could see how hard and large his cock was.

"Daddy's gonna put this inside his little girl now, okay? Just lie there and relax," he spoke as he took his cock in his hand and started pulling it. I liked watching him do this and could hardly wait to have that huge cock inside me. I wanted to feel it stretching me as if I was a little girl. He laid down on top of me, putting the end of his penis at the opening and pushed very slowly until the end was almost inside.

"Oh Daddy, that feels nice. Are you gonna put it in deeper? It's big isn't it Daddy?"

"Yes Sweetie. Daddy's gonna put it all in there," and he pushed a little deeper then pulled it back out again. It did feel like I was a little girl as the head of his massive cock continued to open me up for the rest of it. He continued to push deeper each time and I put my hands on his ass to pull him toward me as he moved in and out. I wanted it as deep as possible, and he finally started to push in all the way. It felt wonderful, so deep inside me and so thick that I was teetering between pleasure and pain as he fucked me.

"That's my good little girl. You like fucking Daddy don't you?"

"Yes Daddy. Fuck me Daddy. I want to feel it squirt inside me please, Daddy," I moaned as he started to move more quickly. "Fuck your little girl, Daddy. Yes, yes." I could feel his cock swelling as his breathing started to become more rapid. Then he pushed in deep and I could feel the pulsations and squirting as he filled me with his cum. When it finally stopped he collapsed on top of me, telling me how wonderful that felt.

"For me too. I enjoyed having your beautiful big cock deep inside me. It was wonderful."

We slowly started to move and he invited me to go ahead and have a shower if I wished as I got up to use the bathroom. The shower was all glass and large enough for an entire family. I enjoyed a quick, hot shower and then put my bra and dress on, purposely leaving my panties on the bed, and meeting Steve downstairs in the kitchen.

"I've called a car for you, Sweetie. It can wait until you're ready to go. He's already been paid with tip. Just give him your address and he'll see you get home safely. It will be the same car and maybe even the same driver that will pick you up any time you wish to go out," he said as he handed me his business card.

# THE BEGINNING

I reached up and kissed him on the cheek. "Thank you for everything. I had a wonderful time."

"As I have too, Tessy. You've done more for me this night than I can describe," he said as he walked me to the front door. I left with a smile on my face, giving directions to the driver as we headed toward the gates.

I was surprised the next afternoon at the bike shop when they brought my new ride out from the back. Not only was it equipped with two cages and water bottles, but a tool kit, and a Garmin bike computer as well.

"I think there's been a mistake, I didn't order those things on my bike," I said in shock. The mechanic looked at the work order that was attached to the bike.

"There's no charge. That's already been paid for yesterday and I see you've already paid for the bike so you're good to go!" he said as he handed me a riding jersey and congratulated me again on my new purchase.

Once I was home and had the bike leaned against one of the walls in my living room, I phoned the number on Steve's card. He answered by saying his name and I began thanking him profusely.

"I wasn't expecting you to do that. Thank you for the generous gifts, Steve!" I exclaimed.

"And thank you for the gift you left me last night," he replied and I remembered I'd left him my panties.

"You're most welcome. I can't wait to get out for a ride again. Next weekend, do you know if you'll be riding?"

"Saturday morning 10am. Meet us at the fountain in the courtyard of the club."

"I'll work really hard this week so I don't have homework Saturday night."

I rarely missed a Saturday morning ride from early in the spring until late in the fall for the next three years when I had finished medical school and moved away. My Saturday evening sessions with Steve gradually slowed from a couple of times per month to once every couple of months as he grew older and seemed to need me less. Nonetheless, I became his little girl whenever we were alone together, his dirty little girl I should say. I fell into it easily and willingly, surprising myself at times with the creativity I showed. I exposed myself to him in public when no one could see so he would spank me later for being naughty. I sat on his lap while he finger fucked me as we relaxed in his hot tub on clear moonlit nights. I rarely slept over, but when I did he would make pancakes and syrup for breakfast and I'd suck his cock again before I left. He continually showered me with gifts and gestures of kindness making it a decadent pleasure being his spoiled little girl.

During the second year of riding together I developed an altogether different relationship with Keith as well. He'd always shown interest in me, but I suppose because of his age, he probably didn't think I would be interested in him. On one Saturday afternoon when Lee and Steve weren't able to join us, Keith started to confide in me during our ride together.

"My wife left this morning for a month to visit her sister in England."

"A month! That's a long time to be apart," I replied.

"Actually we've been apart for the last thirty years or so, Tesh. We live in the same house and socialize together with friends, but we haven't had sex for at least twenty of those years. Once we found out I was unable to have children, she slowly shut down and shut me out. We've had separate bedrooms for twenty years, Tesh."

"I'm sorry to hear that, Keith. That must be difficult for you," I replied. "How have you managed to stay together all these years? What do you do?"

"It has been difficult, but young men learn how to take care of their needs when they don't have a girlfriend and that's simply how it is for me. The reason for staying together is purely financial really. She wants nothing more than friendship from me so we've basically shared a home together, as sad as that is. She doesn't want for anything and we're happy to have our own hobbies and enjoy time together with couples we've known for many years."

We continued our ride, talking about various other topics and at the end of it, he asked me to come to his house for cocktails and a barbecue that night. I knew what he was after and that he would never ask or assume anything, but I eagerly accepted his invitation knowing that I was going to give him what he hadn't had for many years. We parted as usual at the country club and an hour later he picked me up at my apartment and we drove to his house. Keith's home and yard was like something out of a magazine and although it was lovely to look at, I never once felt as though I could relax and enjoy being there. It was too perfect and sterile.

We sipped wine on the back patio while he barbecued steaks. Neither one of us seemed very hungry for food so we quickly put the dishes on the kitchen counter and sat back down on the sectional patio furniture overlooking the manicured flower garden and small fish pond. As he spoke about maintaining their yard, I moved closer and put his hand on my knee. He continued to speak, slowly moving his hand on my leg and then up underneath my skirt, eventually moving it closer and closer to my cunt. I uncrossed my ankles and moved my legs apart so he could touch me. He had stopped talking at this point and I noticed he was trembling slightly.

"Why don't we go inside now," I suggested.

"Yes, yes," he replied, picking up the bottle of wine and leading me into the house. Keith didn't stop at the kitchen and continued down the hallway to his bedroom, sat on the edge of his bed, setting the wine down on the bedside table, and I did the same thing. I stood in front of him and removed my skirt and top, which left me naked. He moved his hands up and down my back and over my breasts, then down over my bum and up and down my legs. I took one step closer and he started to suck on my nipples as his hands continued to explore my ass and then my cunt. I become more excited and spread my feet apart as he put his fingers inside me, slowly moving them in and out. I moved my hands onto the buttons on his shirt and eventually down to his shorts, unbuttoning and unzipping the shorts. We stopped touching one another momentarily while he stood up to remove his shirt and shorts. I noticed his cock wasn't hard yet and decided I'd better get to work on that, thinking he might not be that excited by what we were doing.

"Lie down and enjoy my mouth on your cock for a while," I told him as I gently pushed his chest with my hand. He lay down on the bed allowing me to kneel between his knees and I slowly lowered my mouth onto his semi soft cock. I spent what felt like a long time trying to get him hard, at first sucking softly and putting his cock all the way into my mouth, then using my tongue and stroking the underside of it while I moved my mouth firmly up and down on his shaft, then teasing the end of it with my tongue, then tickling his balls, then licking his balls. I couldn't figure out what he needed me to do in order to get him excited. After a few more minutes he lifted his ass up off the bed and put his hand underneath himself. I continued to move my mouth up and down on his cock as he began rocking back and forth and playing with his asshole. I could feel his cock start to get firmer and within another few minutes I could tell it was going to shoot in my mouth even though it wasn't fully erect. His breathing continued to get more rapid and he seemed to be moving the end of his finger in a circular motion at the entrance of his asshole.

"I'm gonna cum," he gasped at last and when I didn't remove my mouth, he shot his load and I swallowed eagerly. He became soft immediately and I continued to gently stroke it with my mouth and tongue, until he was lying absolutely still. I stretched out on the bed beside him and he reached over with his hand and grabbed my arm.

"That was out of this world. Thank you. I'll die a happy man now," he said gently, squeezing my arm. After a few more minutes, I got up, picked my skirt and top up off the floor and dressed. Keith sat up reaching for his shirt and shorts and then filled our glasses with wine, picking mine up and passing it to me and holding his out towards me.

"You're an incredible woman, Tesh. Cheers."

"Cheers," I replied.

During the month his wife was away, I visited Keith's home several times a week, allowing him to make up for lost time. Although he never really had a hard erection, it was firm enough for penetration and when I put the end of my finger in his asshole, he came almost immediately. I eventually asked him if he'd ever tried a vibrator for stimulating himself and he replied he would be too afraid to have his wife find it. Unfortunate, I thought, that she controlled his pleasure even when she wasn't aware.

Like Steve, my visits with Keith lessened over time also, and when I was near the end of medical school, I felt they might both be weaning themselves from spending intimate moments together. Steve had even started to miss rides and I learned later he had started having health problems that he didn't want any of us to know about. Lee was always friendly and talkative, but I had long suspected his interests sexually were not about having a young woman, but maybe if I were a male, we'd have found common ground.

Our last best day together as a group ended with late afternoon cocktails and appies at Brandy's. I was only months away from becoming a GP, and was already starting to feel the freedom from years of studying and hard work. All three of my amigos reminded me of when we first met three years earlier at the bike shop with their continual teasing of one another and flattery towards me. It had been a great day!

A very fit looking, young man walked up to our table saying he was told we were regular riders. He introduced himself as Ken and proceeded to tell us he'd just moved back from Europe where he'd been making a living as a professional rider.

"Well, nice to meet you Ken, I'm Steve. This is Tesh, Lee and Keith," he gestured to each of us with his introductions, shaking Ken's hand. "Join us," he said and pointed to an empty chair. Ken thanked him, taking a seat and telling us he was interested to know more about the riding community here. We talked briefly about our regular rides and the groups we knew of from the bike shops, and then listened, as Ken thrilled us with his stories of the life of a professional athlete. I was mesmerized and caught up in what a wonderful and different life he had lived compared to the last eight years of mine which was spent with my head in textbooks. I was ripe for someone who was everything I wasn't, and that was Ken.

When it was time for us to leave, Ken looked at his watch and said he should be going as well. I headed toward my recently re-licensed red Volkswagen as Ken walked beside me, continuing to talk.

"Do you want to get something to eat, Tesh? I just realized I haven't eaten since this morning. It's been a busy day for me today."

"Sure," I said. "I'm a student though so all I can afford these days is take-out pizza and beer. Would you like to come over?" I asked.

"That sounds perfect. My ride left earlier. Do you mind if I jump in with you?"

"Not if you don't mind riding in my old VW," I replied.

I might have noticed that somehow I paid for both pizza and beer had I not been completely mesmerized by the words he spoke to me that evening. It was if I had become the enchanted princess, listening intently to my prince as he professed his love and admiration for my beauty, only he wasn't just speaking of my beauty, and making me feel special, but was also extracting the information he wanted from me. He told me how much he'd like to ride with me and that he'd give me some tips that would make my riding easier. He commented on my obvious athleticism which would make coaching me a pleasure. He asked about my childhood, my family, my dreams and goals once I was finished medical school. I was easily hooked, anxious to hear his stories of adventure and racing, and easily influenced into believing he was interested in me. He joked that he didn't have much besides his bikes but that he didn't have debt like I must have. I told him that in fact with the recent passing of my dad, I was fortunate to be without student loans or debt of any type. I told him I had already been talking to a realtor about buying a place. I'd soon be able to have a home of my own which I hadn't had since leaving my parents' house years earlier. It was those words, that information that turned dinner into his spending the night and every night thereafter. When he moved in a few weeks later, I hardly noticed. His belongings were little more than a gym bag and his well-used road bike. It was with the skill and cunning of a con artist rather than a professional athlete that enabled the penniless opportunist to become what I believed was the prince of my dreams.

Our relationship moved along very quickly and before I knew it, he was suggesting I start my practice in Brighton, which happened to be close to his parents.

"It would be a smart move, Tessy, especially if we want to think about getting married and starting a family."

I couldn't believe my ears!

# THE BEGINNING

"Get married and start a family! Oh Ken, that would be wonderful. Yes, yes, yes!" I exclaimed as tears ran down my cheeks. I thought I'd finally found my prince!

I immediately started planning and hoped Johnny would fly home to give me away at my wedding. It was more like throw me to the wolves than give me away, but at the time I was blinded by what I thought was my dream come true.

Brighton wasn't what I'd originally planned as a location for starting my practice, but it made sense when he described starting a family in a smaller community and being close to relatives. My parents were gone and Johnny was teaching English in China, who knows where he might wind up and now that Ken was planning to become a realtor, he thought it would be easier to get to know people in a smaller community rather than a big city.

Ken had soon found the "perfect" location for me to start my practice because I could buy the building and make money renting the other space out, which would pay for my location, too, he told me. I found it rather strange that he'd looked at houses near his parents and a commercial building without mentioning it to me. When I asked he said I was far too busy to worry about those details.

"I'll take care of all that stuff, Tessy. It's what I'm good at," he assured me.

I knew Brighton didn't need another doctor, but I knew in time I could build my practice. It was a struggle at first while Ken was taking his realtor course and I was working extra shifts at the drop-in clinic, but within a couple of years, I was as busy as I could be and Ken eventually got a couple of listings. The building I'd bought for my practice was in a good location, but the rental space was difficult to keep rented and hadn't been paying for itself nor had the mortgage on the building like Ken thought. When I asked Ken about this he replied sharply.

"Tessy, it's all good. I know what I'm doing."

A month later when I noticed Ken had depleted $75,000.00, the last of the money that remained of my inheritance, I confronted him again about our debt.

"I'm managing our debt Tessy and I needed that money to get my business off the ground and buy a proper vehicle for myself. I can't drive around in a junker! Are you saying it's not our money?" he asked in a tone that suggested I was keeping something from him.

"No Ken!" I replied. "But $75,000.00 is a lot of money and we should be discussing this prior to your making a unilateral decision. That's all I'm saying," I pleaded.

He stormed out of the house, leaving me feeling as though I was the one that had damaged our relationship somehow. I apologized later that day.

Ken thought it was best if we bought a new house rather than go through the expense of renovating, and we wound up paying much more than we had budgeted because he insisted we needed to locate ourselves in a certain area of the city. I started to feel some of the strains of our finances and suggested we do some calculations. We had a mortgage on our house, a mortgage on the commercial building for my practice as well as insurances, payroll for my staff and all the other expenses of running my practice and his business which was yet to support itself. I thought we should think about starting a family, but Ken reassured me that everything would work out, children would come along with time, and he needed more time to establish himself and develop relationships with important people in town. I was tired, and often felt as though I was working all the time while Ken had established a weekly afternoon of golf and often played on the weekend as well. Although he had more time on his hands than I did, he didn't take on any of the tasks of running the household. He argued I was more aware of what needed to be done and that by the time he might notice the laundry needed doing, which was when he was out of clean socks, I would have already done it. He didn't like to grocery shop or cook and would suggest we pick up pizza or go out for sushi when I didn't have something organized for dinner. I found it easier to forge ahead than to spend energy fighting. Ken was a master at turning our fights around and making it sound like I was measuring our relationship on who did what for whom. I always came away from those arguments feeling as though I was asking too much.

When the girls eventually did come along, I hardly had a moment to spare. We employed a nanny for the first few years so I could return to work after three months. There's no maternity leave when you're self-employed and Ken said we needed the income. The nanny was a big help with the twins, but the organization of her, the groceries, cooking, and activities for the kids continued to fall on my plate. Ken was busier with real estate, but it came with the expectation that he golf more, buy a membership at the country club, attend social gatherings, and take clients to see homes on the weekends. It was true he never complained about working on the weekend, but it was also true that his work never interfered with his golf game either.

We bought a boat when the girls were both in school. Ken insisted it would be an excellent activity for us as a family and we would all be able to escape work together on the weekend.

"Ken, I don't think we should take on boat payments on top of what we already have on our plate."

"We can afford it, Tesh. It's no problem and this is for our family. We'll have so much fun together with the girls. We deserve this, Tessy. Especially you, you need to get away and relax on the weekend and when you're at home you can't seem to stop doing stuff."

I'll never forget the conversation we had a few months later when he told me we needed a second mortgage on our home.

"The real estate market is a bit slow right now, Tesh. We need this extra cash until the spring when things will start to pick up again. It always does. This will allow us to make our payments and continue to live the way we should live."

"What do you mean, Ken? What's changed? Have we not been able to make our payments or something? I thought we were still doing okay."

"Well the commercial property has never been able to support itself. The cost of the renovations on the building was higher than we budgeted and took a bigger bite out of the line of credit. I use the line of credit to pay my agency fees every month and so yes we're short every month making our commitments, Tesh. It's just the way it is. We have equity in the house and we can use that for another line of credit. We'll manage."

I was stunned. We were in worse financial shape than I thought and yet we had a boat.

"We need to sell something, Ken. We can't do this."

"No Tesh. Selling doesn't make sense in this market. We need to use our equity to borrow until the market improves. That's what we need to do. This is what I do, Tesh. Trust me, I know what I'm doing here. I've looked at all the trends and this is the best thing for us to do."

"We should sell the boat Ken. That's an expense of $450.00 per month that we don't need. Your golf costs double that per month and those two expenditures we could do without," I protested.

"We'll never sell the boat for the amount of the loan so we'll still be paying the loan and won't have the enjoyment of the boat either, Tesh. I won't sell the boat. I need to golf with clients, Tesh. You know that. We have equity in our home and that's what we need to access now."

I eventually signed the second line of credit, fearful that if I didn't, my marriage was doomed. I couldn't bear the thought of losing my family. Instead I ignored the screaming in my gut and worked harder, taking on a regular evening shift again at a local walk-in clinic. My days at the office were becoming more difficult because my nights were restless. I knew my marriage was falling apart before my eyes and that we were in debt to the point of bankruptcy if something wasn't done soon.

# CHAPTER 7
## Phone Call

"Finally!" I think, as my cell phone rings with the ring that alerts me Tom was calling.

"Hi Baby!" he says after I answer. "I miss you so much. How was work today? I don't think you'll recognize me, I haven't shaved since I've been away."

"I miss you too. Oh I think I'll recognize you no problem. The kitchen is a mess. I promise I'll have it all straightened up before you're back."

"Don't touch any of it. I'll never find anything if you do it. Just leave it for me, Baby."

"*What's wrong my Powerful One?*" asks Magnus before I have a chance to say anything more to Tom.

"I'm going through the old photos, reliving memories, and Tom just reminded me of one when he said he hadn't shaved. It was a time when I was thirteen that I care not to remember."

"*Remember Powerful One, it is not wise to keep things in as you know.*"

"I know," I reply.

*"Then speak it now."*

"It was toward the end of my summer break when my friend Sherry invited me to go into town for the day to hang out while her Mom shopped. We'd done this many times before on the weekend and it was always fun to have a change of scenery and something new to do. Sherry's mom gave us the talk before letting us go for the day.

"And what do you do if someone approaches you?"

"We run!" Sherry and I say together.

"That's right, no talking to strangers and stay together no matter what. This isn't the same as being at home. I'll see you at the meeting spot girls."

And with that we were off for a day of fun and adventure, first hanging out at the park where many of the kids from town would play during the summer holidays. We entertained ourselves on the swing set and monkey bars before progressing to window shopping on one of the main streets after buying a drink at the corner store with our spending money. We met Sherry's mom for lunch at our usual lunch spot, excited that we were both allowed to have a cheeseburger, french fries and share a chocolate milkshake. Both of us cheered when Mrs. Gallway told us she needed another hour or so to finish her shopping and errands before heading for home.

"What's your favorite music?" Sherry asked after a car drove past, loudly playing the latest Eagles album. "I really like Hotel California."

"Ya, me too," I replied secretly wishing I was listening from inside the car that had just passed with its wide tires and flames down the side.

"That's a really cool car, too," Sherry pointed.

"I can hardly wait until I have my driver's license," I replied, wishing my youth away.

Before long we met up with Mrs. Gallway at our designated location and spent the next hour grocery shopping before heading for home.

"I'm just gonna stop at the house and unload these groceries first, Tessy, or the ice cream will melt," Mrs. Gallway tells me. As we pull into their yard, I decide I'd rather walk home than wait for her to unpack all the groceries before driving me home.

"I'm gonna walk home okay? It doesn't take me that long."

"Are you sure, Tessy? I can drive you as soon as I take these groceries out."

"It's okay, I'll walk. Thank you for taking me. I had a really good time."

We say our good-byes and I begin the trek to our farm which generally takes me about forty-five minutes if I keep up a good pace. Just past the half way mark I start wishing I'd waited for a ride, not realizing how tired I'd become after a day in town. A funny looking white van pulls up beside me and slows down. I hear loud music playing and the driver yells out the window at me.

"Hi. Would ya' be wantin' a ride or would ya' be walkin'?" the driver asks in a funny accent if he's read my mind as he turns down the music.

"Oh yes, thank you. I would," I say with relief. "I live at the end of Wyant Road, that way," I point down the road.

"Eye, I know that area! Jump in then. I'll be takin' ya' there," he tells me and stops the van.

I run around the front of the van and get in the passenger side.

"Buckle up," he tells me and I feel like I'm about to take a ride with my Dad. I notice the van has a drape behind the front seats that stops me from seeing what's in the back. I was a bit disappointed as I'd never been in a van like this before. He continues down the road, but takes a turn to the right, heading down the dirt road that doesn't go anywhere. I wonder why he's gone this way all of a sudden.

"This road doesn't go all the way through. You have to go the other way."

"Don't worry," he tells me. "I'll be stoppin' just up here for a moment," and continues driving, parking a few minutes later at the edge of the bush. After he turns off the motor he tells me to come and see the back of the van.

"I won't hurt ya'," he tells me as he pulls the drape across. "C'mon now!" he instructs, motioning with his arm and I undue my seat belt and enter the back of the van.

"*What happened next?*" Magnus asked when I paused for a moment. I took a deep breath and continued with my story.

"The back of the van was like a little camper. It had a fridge, stove, cupboards and a bed. He told me to sit down on the bed and reached into the fridge to get a beer for himself and a coke for me.

"It's not much, but she be my home," he said. "Go on now, have a drink. You be thirsty from walkin'?"

I took a drink of coke and looked at the man who was now sitting on the other end of the bed. His hair was long, black and gray coloured, and needed to be combed. His face was wrinkly and it looked like he was growing a beard or hadn't shaved for days. The gray t-shirt he wore had holes around the neck and belly and his jeans were faded and torn. He set his beer down on the small counter next to the fridge and continued to speak.

"Ya' don't need to be afraid of me. I won't hurt ya'. I'm gonna be showin' ya' a little somethin' so you should be payin' attention," and with that he knelt on the floor in front of me and put his hand on my chest, gently pushing me back onto the bed. As I laid back with my legs over the edge of the bed, he pulled my shorts and panties down to my ankles and over my shoes. He kept telling me to relax as he pushed my legs up and out until I was fully exposed to him. I turned my head, closed my eyes, and wondered how I could ever relax.

"That's a sweet lookin' little thing and it smells lovely," he said and I felt his breath on the inside of my legs as he kissed my thighs and belly. I tried to pull my legs together, but his body was large and I had no strength against his size. He continued to kiss me, working his way down between my legs until he was licking inside my pussy and around my ass. I couldn't believe he wanted to lick me down there and enjoyed smelling it, too. I wondered if everyone did this?

Then I felt his finger moving around my asshole and gently pushing on the outside as he continued to lick me. I tightened my bum and tried to close my legs again, but couldn't. He moved his finger away from my asshole to my pussy and then slowly pushed it inside. I could feel a pleasurable sensation of licking on the outside as he gently put his finger in and out. This wasn't anything like what I'd been doing with Ben who moved very quickly once his cock was inside me. His finger felt the same as Ben's cock, but it moved very slowly and I could feel what was happening. As he did this, he rubbed me on my legs and up underneath my shirt with his other hand and it felt warm, but rough against my skin. He was very gentle and slow while he did these things to me unlike Ben or Daren who seemed to be finished within seconds. I wondered if he was enjoying what he was doing down there. When he slowly stopped the probing and then the licking, I continued to lie still, but opened my eyes to see that he was removing his clothes. I noticed his penis was soft, but was much bigger than Daren's and I felt sick inside my stomach wondering if he might want to put that inside me. His balls were covered with hair and swayed back and forth when he removed his pants. It reminded me of the bulls on the farm when they ran and their big set of balls would swing back and forth beneath them. He was naked now and pulled me toward him by grasping my hands and pulling.

"We'll be tryin' somethin' diffrent now," he said as I sat up on the bed. "Go ahead and play with that," he told me as he spread his legs and exposed his cock. It didn't look anything like Ben's or

Daren's. There appeared to be no head on the end of it, just skin. As I put my hand on it, he placed his hand on top of mine, squeezed it around his cock, then started moving our hands up and down on the shaft. He put my other hand underneath his balls.

"Play with them," he told me. "Gentle there. That's the family jewels you've got in yer hand now."

I had grabbed his balls tightly at first, thinking it would be like the cock, but cradled them when he flinched and told me to be gentle. As I fondled with one hand and we stroked with the other, I could tell he was getting excited. I noticed the end of his cock starting to come farther out the end each time as it began to get hard. I couldn't take my eyes off his hand on the cock as it moved slowly but continuously up and down. When he told me to put my mouth on it, I moved between his legs but was only able to put the end of it in my mouth. He took his hand off mine and I expected to feel it move to my head, but he caressed my back instead. My hand didn't go all the way around his cock any longer because it had become big and hard, but I continued to move it slowly up and down while my mouth was on the end. He took my other hand, put my index finger in his mouth and started to move his tongue along my finger while slowly moving my finger in and out of his mouth. He was trying to show me what to do with my mouth on his penis rather than pushing my head up and down and gagging me. As I started to move my head on the end of his cock, he moved my finger in and out of his mouth with the same motion. He put my finger to the end of his mouth and circled it with his tongue, then pushed my finger deep, pulling it back out slightly when it reached his throat. I moved my head on his cock and used my tongue as he was doing although I found it difficult to put it very deep inside. As I gently played with his balls I could feel his cock get even harder and he even moaned when I did this. After a few minutes, he put his hand back on top of mine and started to move it up and down on his cock. I took my mouth off the end to watch and he immediately started to move his hand quickly. I liked seeing the head of his cock move in and out of the skin and I knew what was soon going to happen. I could feel his balls tightening.

"Here it comes now," he said and I put my head back down close to the end and when I thought he was getting the pained look on his face I put my mouth on his cock and it immediately started to shoot. He continued to stroke it gently and slowly until I had swallowed it all down. I kept my mouth on his cock even after he'd taken his hand away, noticing the end felt silky soft to my tongue and the skin was nice to pull into my mouth. After a few moments more, I took my hand away from his balls and removed my mouth from his cock.

"That was lovely. What do ya' think?"

"It was good," I replied as I reached for my panties and shorts.

"Yer very beautiful and ye taste good."

I had never heard these words before. I didn't know what to say.

"Thank you. Can I go home now?"

"Yes ye can," he said as he pulled his jeans on and slipped his shirt over his head. He moved to the front of the van and I followed, taking my place in the passenger seat and buckling my seat belt. He started the van and drove toward the main road, turning towards home and let me out just shy of the driveway.

"If ye were payin' attention, this will help ye get where yer goin'," he told me as I was opening the door. I didn't understand what he meant, but I said thank you anyway. I closed the door and ran toward the house without looking back toward the road.

"I've never spoken of this to anyone, Magnus. I'm surprised at how much detail I was able to recall, it's been buried inside me for many years. I thought it was my fault for taking the ride with a stranger."

"*I know this. Do you remember what happened the next time you saw the boys?*"

# THE BEGINNING

"Well I don't remember seeing Ben again that summer, but I do remember being with Daren."

"*You remember?*"

"Yes, I remember him pulling his cock out as he always did, but when he put his hand toward my head, I pushed it away and put my mouth on his cock myself and started to suck. I moved my tongue around the end of his cock and along the back of the shaft as I slowly moved my mouth up and down. When I was able to do it myself, I found I could put the whole thing in my mouth without choking. After using my mouth for a while, I started to fondle his balls while I sucked. I felt the excitement building inside him and I remember both of us were moaning softly this time. His breath became more shallow and quick, and he moaned loudly just before he moved and lost his balance, which made his cock came out of my mouth. He shot his cum onto the ground and a little bit landed on my jeans. When he started to zip up and was looking out the window, I tried to wipe the cum up with my finger, but it had already soaked in. I remember feeling disappointed that I'd done that on my own and didn't get to taste the cum that day, but he seemed nervous and rushed to get us out of the wood shed. I remember being with him again, but it wasn't there. Why did I never go back to the wood shed?"

*"Very good. Relax now. We will speak of this again soon. Focus on positive, leave the photos for now if it's bothering you,"* he instructs. *"I will let the aerial out."*

"I don't understand. Why didn't I go back to the wood shed?"

*"Leave it! I will not speak this again,"* he responds sharply and I know not to push.

Tom's familiar teasing voice brings me back to reality as he tells me about some fictitious adventure he'd had that day as he so often does when he wants to make me laugh.

"Oh Tom, I miss you so much," I say choking back emotion as I suddenly realize again how difficult it is for me to be away from him.

"I miss you way more," he replies as he always does, telling me with matter of fact certainty that he loves me more or misses me more than I could ever imagine. Magnus tells me the same, saying that I haven't even felt the depth of the aerial's love yet. It blows me away to think that I could actually be loved this way. I find it hard to grasp after searching for this all my life, feeling nothing but disappointment and resolving that my idea of love is something found in fairy tales and fantasy novels. No wonder I get sick each time it is taken away from me, even if it's simply for a few hours or a couple of days.

"The rest of the family gets here tomorrow and then the funeral is Thursday afternoon. We've pretty much got it all sorted now."

We exchange a few more words and then I make the mistake of yawning. He almost ends the conversation immediately telling me to go straight to bed so I won't be too tired for work in the morning.

"You need to rest up so you're not sleeping all weekend when I'm back, Tesh. You work too hard now git! Love you," and with that he hangs up the phone.

I head straight into the bathroom and get ready for bed, then give Rex her customary cat treats while lying in bed. This is a habit I'd started long ago when I was trying to get Rex to come when I called her. She still won't come when I call, but a quick shake of the treat bag and she's beside me in a heartbeat. Damn cat. I love her to pieces.

As always, morning seems to come all too quickly and I wake with an uneasy feeling. As I start to stir, Rex makes her way onto the bed and up to my face for her morning scratch and snuggle. She is a welcome distraction to the anxious feelings that have plagued me these last couple of years, especially on those mornings when Tom and I don't wake together. Sometimes I have a vague memory of a dream, but for the most part, they vanish before

I have a chance to try and understand what it was that made me upset. But enough of that, Rex's insistent rubbing and meowing indicates it's time for cream, and I jump up, stumble over the pillows on the floor and head for the bathroom. With Rex darting between my feet, I focus on getting to the toilet and relax for a few extra moments, allowing her to rub across my legs while I stroke her head and back.

"Guess what day it is, Rexxy? It's Thursday, and that means Daddy comes home tomorrow!" I exclaim opening the heavy glass door and entering the shower.

"That feels better. I'm awake now, Rex."

Wrapping a towel around my waist, I enter the kitchen and fill a bowl with cream, carefully avoiding Rex's attempts to rub her head on the dish as I place it on the floor.

"This place is a bloody mess!"

I quickly apply a bit of eye shadow and mascara, comb my hair and decide to tie it back in a ponytail, allowing a few wavy pieces to frame my face. I notice how the sun bleached streaks that I've had since childhood have turned from blond to platinum over these past several years. I pack my work clothes and change of shoes into the pannier and head out on my bike. My first stop is *Witch Brew?* for the first cup of water today that tastes good.

## THE BEGINNING

Carol greets me as I arrive via the back door to the office, telling me I have a packed day with a few extras squeezed in. I lean my bike in the back hall next to my office and our staff bathroom while Carol continues to talk. She stands just less than five feet tall, with jet black, closely cropped hair, beautiful blue eyes and a warm smile. Today wearing pink pastel scrubs that hug her slightly plump figure, Carol consistently runs the office with complete efficiency and respect, favouring no one patient over another. I cherish her matter of fact demeanour and quick wit.

"Full moon in a couple days, Boss, the crazies are comin' outta the woodwork already," She jokes. "First appointment is already sitting in room one, but you've got five more minutes."

I nod in agreement about the full moon. Everyone in law enforcement and the medical profession knows it gets busier in the emergency room and often in our offices around that time.

"Damn I forgot my lunch!" I say out loud as I unpack my pannier. I quickly finish dressing in my work clothes, hang my riding gear in the bathroom at the back of the office, pick up my laptop and head into room one. The morning moves along smoothly as I meticulously assess, advise and prescribe to each of my patients. We stay on time despite the couple of extra patients and lonely regulars that find an excuse to book appointments on a regular basis and by twelve ten, Carol locks the door for our lunch break. As I head toward my office she informs me Tom is waiting on line one.

My heart skips a beat and I'm immediately concerned with this uncharacteristic occurrence.

"Hi Hunny, I miss you so much. Is everything okay?"

"I miss you more, Baby. I'm sorry for calling you at the office, but I had a call from Josh this morning. He's coming here this weekend for his cousin's wedding and heard I was here. He asked if I'd stick around and spend some time with him. I got the feeling there's something up. I can change my flight, unfortunately with a small fee, but I think I should stay to see him, Baby."

"Of course! That's no problem. Let me know when you change your flight."

"I love you. I'll let you get back to work, Baby. Make sure you eat some lunch now."

And with that, we say our good-byes and hang up. Disappointed, but hungry, I walk into the staff room and pick up an apple from the bowl of fruit in the middle of the table.

"Oh no, what's wrong?" Carol asks looking up from her magazine. I've never been able to hide anything from Carol who tells me I'm as easy to read as the morning paper.

"Tom's extending his trip," I moan as I drop down onto the small love-seat. "I know I shouldn't be upset, it's only a couple more days and it's because he has the opportunity to spend some time with the boy he helped raise, but I can't help feeling disappointed. I miss him so much, Carol."

"Ya know what, Doc?" Carol starts gently, closing her magazine. "It's incredibly sweet to the point of sickening how much you two love each other. If my old man went outta' town I'd be celebrating! Watchin' chick flicks and eatin' take-out, I'd love it, but you mope around like a fresh weaned puppy. Go finish some of those charts while I go out and grab a wrap for ya'. It helps to keep your mind busy."

"Thanks Carol," I reply with a sigh as I follow her instructions, first checking my email to see Tom's already sent an updated agenda.

"Four more days! It's okay," I reassure myself. "I will survive. Maybe I'll watch *Chocolat* again tonight."

My afternoon is every bit as busy as the morning with a couple of appointments taking longer than usual.

"Hello Mr. Jones," I greet a former colleague of Ken's that's been a patient of mine since I opened my practice here. "Let's start by taking your blood pressure. It's been awhile since you've been in the office. Retirement going well?"

"Well I'd be enjoying it more if I wasn't getting up a couple times a night to pee," he starts.

"Things aren't working as well as they used to either."

"Your blood pressure is a little high and I see you've gained a few pounds since last time. I don't want to give you anything for the blood pressure, but you might want to give up the golf cart and start walking more so this doesn't escalate. It's important that we get this under control. I'll get something for the other from the sample cupboard," I say before leaving for a moment. Mr. Jones appears a bit embarrassed as I lay the two boxes of medication down on the counter in front of him.

"Take one daily for the next month. It may take a couple of weeks or more before you notice an improvement in those symptoms with your bladder, but the other issue should be back to normal within about five days. The medication is generally well tolerated and I'll see you in a month." I tell him as I hand him a patient information pamphlet on benign prostatic hypertrophy and another on erectile dysfunction.

"Any questions?"

"No thank you. I'll make another appointment." he says as he stands to leave.

I carry my laptop into the next room where a young teenager wearing tight skinny jeans and a tube top is waiting with her mother.

"Hello Ladies," I say as I enter. "What can I help with today?"

"I think Brittany might have a bladder infection," the mother, Susan, tells me.

"Is everyone comfortable talking openly here?" I ask before continuing.

"Of course!" Susan exclaims.

"Can I see Dr. Peterson alone Mom?" Brittany says with an air of attitude in her voice.

"Oh okay. We'll talk later then," Susan says as she leaves the room, closing the door behind her."

"The sample didn't show a bladder infection, Brittany, but I'm wondering if there might be something else going on," I start. "Do you have a boyfriend?"

"Yes."

"Are you having sex with him?"

"Yes, but only a couple of times," she answers defensively.

"You didn't use a condom?" I ask.

"Only the first time. He said he didn't like wearing it and he'd be careful to pull out," she replies, tears welling in her eyes.

"I believe he gave you a sexually transmitted disease, Brittany, but we need to do a different test to be sure. When was your last period?"

"I don't remember. What kind of test?"

"We send a sample to the lab. I think we should do a pregnancy test, too. Should I let you have a few minutes alone to tell your Mom or would you rather I do that?"

"Can you call her in and tell her now?" she says and starts to cry.

I inform Susan and then examine Brittany before letting Carol know we need another sample which proves positive for pregnancy. I take a minute to decide which news to start with, the pregnancy, the suspicion of sexually transmitted disease or the fact that we'd need to ensure all sexual contacts of Brittany and the young boyfriend are informed and treated if positive, then I enter the room again. I leave after we've discussed the immediate plans for Brittany, all of which seemed to crush the attitude of arrogance that was with her when she arrived in my office that day.

The last appointment of the day is no easier.

"I'm separating from Rod. We just decided and it's been really ugly. I need something to help me sleep," Judy tells me as we start her appointment.

As I quickly look through Judy's current medications and recent appointments from the drop-in clinic, I realize there's probably more to this story.

"I'm very sorry to hear that, Judy. What do you mean by ugly?" I ask.

"He found out I was having an affair so everything ended abruptly. He's very angry and hurt and is making my life hell of course. This truly wasn't the way I wanted it to work out, but Chuck and I are in love. I would have told him earlier, but we had the family reunion with everyone coming. It had been planned for so long. I couldn't ruin it for him and the kids."

"I see. Are you in the home with the kids or …?"

"No he's with them in the house and I'm at a friend's until Chuck and I can get set up. Chuck has kids too so we're both really feeling stressed about it all at the moment. I can fall asleep but I wake up in the night and I start thinking about everything and I can't fall asleep again. I just need something to get me through these next couple of weeks and I'll be fine."

"This can be one of the most stressful events for families, Judy. Have you taken some time off work?"

"Yes, yes I can take as much as I need there fortunately. I've taken a month for now."

"What about alcohol, Judy. We've talked before about your difficulty making good choices when you're drinking," I continue to address my immediate concerns with her, giving her only enough medication for ten nights and asking that she make a follow up appointment with me after that. After she leaves, Carol and I briefly discuss our concerns about Judy and her situation.

"I knew she'd eventually get caught again and who could expect him to be forgiving this time around?" Carol starts as she enters my office. "I'm just glad she didn't give him something these last couple of years."

"If she calls and needs an appointment urgently, we'll need to get her in. I'm concerned this might uncover some of her bigger issues, Carol," I reply.

"I agree Doc. I'll make sure everyone knows. Pretty classic for bipolar disorder don't you think?"

"Yes, and it's unfortunate that most lose everything before they eventually get treatment," I reply as Carol leaves to finish up for the day. Just as we're about ready to leave, Carol meets me in the hallway.

"Doesn't look like tomorrow is gonna be any easier, Boss. Elaine Conch is the first appointment of the day and she's just been told she's full of cancer."

"Oh dear, just when she thought she had cheated death," I sigh as I grab the riding gear off the back of the washroom door, closing it behind me.

Once home, I spend the next few minutes giving Rex her usual helping of love and attention before a quick shower and a search through the freezer for something to eat.

# THE BEGINNING

"Looks like veggie lasagna with meat tonight, Rex," I laugh as I recall Tom's humour about vegetarians and pop the dish in the microwave.

"I can't hold out for another four days and using plastic cutlery and paper plates isn't good for the environment either," I say as I start loading the dishwasher and wiping the countertops.

# CHAPTER 8
## The Path

As I sit on the love-seat eating my lasagna and flipping through a three day old newspaper, I replay the office visit today with my patient Judy. I shake my head as I think how unaware she is of what she's done to her husband and two young kids. The last time he found out she was having an affair they seemed to be able to move beyond her indiscretion, but soon after she told Carol and I both she never really stopped having sexual encounters with several other men. Her overuse of alcohol and other substances, her previous reports of a decreased need for sleep and now the continual promiscuity were diagnostic criteria for bipolar disorder, but Judy had repeatedly refused to address any of it. She had been on antidepressants for years and was gainfully employed so I didn't push too hard beyond one attempt to reach her. Carol was blunt in her approach.

"Judy, ya know what my Dad used to tell me? Ya play with the bull, ya get the horn."

Unfortunately, Judy seemed as oblivious to what the consequences might be then as she was now; callously dismissing the impact this could have on absolutely everyone in her family, including herself. It was unnerving.

I spoke to Magnus about Judy a month or so ago because I was finding it difficult to be her physician and accept what she was doing to her family. He advised me on how I might speak to her, to try and help her by changing her thoughts and getting her back on her path.

"Judy, what do you think will happen when Rod finds out you're doing this?"

She thought for a brief moment and I was hopeful, until she replied, "I don't know. I don't know, but I do know he'll never leave me. He couldn't survive on his own." She dismissed my question with a wave of her hand.

"Do you think you might consider some counselling? If you can't find intimate satisfaction within your marriage, maybe there's a need for a discussion about an alternative lifestyle. I'm not promoting this, but," I tried, but was interrupted.

"Oh he gets lots of blow jobs and fucking from me. Rod doesn't do without that's for sure," she laughed. "That's not it. The guys I'm seeing, I really think I want to make a difference in their lives too. I enjoy hearing about their families. I'm never jealous and I give them what they need. They tell me how much they appreciate it. That makes me feel so good. Last week one of my friends was in town. She and her husband split up six months ago after twenty-five years of marriage. She was devastated when it ended and is now just starting to live again so I got her laid by Chuck's brother. She said she was glad the lights were out because he did nothing for her with his looks, but the sex was great. He went down on her and she told me the next day her ex had never gone down on her once in the twenty-five years they were married. Isn't that sad Dr. Peterson?"

"Yes, it's sad that she never spoke to her husband about oral sex in their twenty-five years of marriage, Judy. That is my point actually. If couples discuss their intimate lives and work together to keep the fires burning, they can prevent the eventual destruction of a family. Love needs to be nurtured, not taken for granted. I'm afraid you've lost sight of that, Judy."

"I know what I'm doing, Dr. Peterson, don't you worry about me. I'm fine," She said in a stern voice ending my attempt to reach her.

When I described the conversation to Magnus later that evening, he told me to just leave it then. We would not try again. He explained how negative builds within, eventually taking over one's thoughts and blinding them to their actions. She had convinced herself, like many do, that what she was doing would be accepted by her husband, her kids, and everyone else. He said the negative was too strong and the gift that had been offered to her by the positive energy, meaning my help, was refused. I told him I felt guilty because I was angry at her, disgusted by her and even wished her to suffer for what she was doing. I thought I was being unprofessional, negative and hypocritical because I had slept with married men at one time myself, but he explained otherwise.

*"Once again you must remember, my Powerful One, most took from you. They lied to you. You are correct, it was wrong, but you were not on your path then. Every day people like Judy are deceitful and greedy. They lie to themselves, denying that what they're doing is harmful and hurtful to others, to the ones that love them. Nothing good comes from something bad and they will always get caught eventually. She is throwing love away. She denied help. She will lose everything now,"* he summarized.

When Magnus asked later if she reminded me of anyone that had done similar to me, it was like an awakening. I immediately understood why I was finding it so difficult to be objective with Judy. I recalled a time three years earlier when I first met Sandy Gregory.

"So nice to finally meet you, Tesh! Ken talks about you all the time. I have trouble keeping him focused on real estate," she laughed as she looked around the pool deck. "You have a beautiful home, very appropriate for someone of your stature, I might add."

"My stature?" I ask embarrassed at the suggestion.

"Are you taking new patients, Tesh? I'm trying to find a female physician in town."

"No, I'm not at present. Sorry."

"Oh there's Rudy! Excuse me, nice meeting you, Tesh."

Sandy attended several of our pool parties, each time speaking to me about how well Ken was doing in the real estate market in Brighton.

"He's just so brilliant with numbers, Tesh. You must be proud, and look at this beautiful spread he's got you in. He works harder than most at real estate. I don't think there's a moment in the day when he's not thinking about how he can make that next sale happen," she gushed the second or third time we'd met. He had certainly sold me a bill of goods I thought. I noticed how she had become more physically affectionate toward Ken as well. He was his usual host with the most during those parties, hugging and touching everyone, but I knew he liked her too. His smug look and Cheshire cat smile made it obvious to me. It wasn't until after we were separated that I understood the extent of their relationship.

The advances by the two other men during previous parties suddenly made complete sense. I seemed to be the only one that wasn't aware of Ken and Sandy's affair. Whether it was out of sympathy toward me or simply seeing a potential opportunity for themselves, Ken's friends had shown me they would be happy to fuck me because he was getting it somewhere else.

Sandy had started to win the girls over even before we were separated, buying them gifts and fussing over them each time she came to one of our parties. Although the light bulb didn't go on for me at that point, when the girls were tight lipped about their weekend at Daddy's friends' cottage within the first couple of weeks we were separated, I suspected where they'd been.

"Bella you told Mommy you were going to a cottage. Did you have fun?"

"It was okay. I don't wanna talk about it anymore."

"I remember going to the cottage when I was your age. We swam in the lake and had campfires? I loved it! Did you have a campfire?"

"Oh yes, Mommy. We had so much fun. I wanna go back so bad, but Daddy told us not to tell you or you wouldn't let us go to Sandy's place ever again!" she blurted, starting to cry, "She bought us floating matts for the lake and everything, Mommy. Please don't say we can't go again. Please."

That was just the beginning of the manipulation of the girls by the very person that should be protecting the relationship they have with their mother yet he was already trying to destroy it so that he might suck them into believing another woman could love them more. One thing I guess I did underestimate about Ken was what a good salesman he truly was.

Sandy proved to be a good salesman, too. Although Ken's parents could be considered "an easy sell" I suppose, as what parent wouldn't want to hear how wonderful their son or daughter was at their chosen profession? Sandy was good at pumping up Ken's reputation as a realtor, and Magnus described the Poison One and his family as negative attracting more negative, all holding hands in a circle to create what they believe is happiness, the best thing, but it's just the opposite in fact. What they're creating is more and more negative energy, taking them farther and farther from their path.

"Jeezuz!" I say out loud as I find myself being dragged back into the battlefields of my mind. "Let's get out of those trenches eh Rex?" I say as I stand up, carrying my dirty dishes back to the kitchen only to drop them into the now empty sink.

"Let's watch a girly movie in bed!" I exclaim as I pick the *Chocolat* DVD out of the cabinet in the living room and head for the bedroom.

"Carol would be proud of me!"

Tom calls the next morning as I'm about to leave for the office. We talk briefly about the funeral and his plans for the day. It's a quick but reassuring call and a wonderful start to the day. I arrive for work with a sense of renewed energy and enthusiasm for life, being one more day closer to Tom's homecoming. It's as if Carol is reading the morning paper again as she watches me walk through the back door with a smile on my face.

"Only three more sleeps eh Doc?" she says placing her hands on her hips and wiggling slightly as an excited puppy might when it sees its owner.

I smile and nod my head, heading into the bathroom to change and clean up for the first patient of the day. Mr. Conch stands beside his wife while she dabs her eyes as I walk into the examining room having quickly scanned the report and recommendations from the cancer centre.

"I can't believe it's back," she sobs. "It's not in my good lung you know."

"They say there's no hope for a cure, just slowing the cancer. I can't believe it. What are we to do?" Mr. Conch demands.

"There must be something. Another study? Some new medications? Please Dr. Peterson, you have to help me. I don't want to die now," begs Mrs. Conch.

I reach for her hand and give it a squeeze recalling the visit she made to my office about a year prior to today.

"I thought I might see you at the cancer centre fundraiser this past weekend, Elaine. Were you there?"

"No, no. My daughter-in-law wanted to buy us tickets, but those things bring back such painful memories that I just can't face going to things like that."

"Painful memories? But you're a cancer survivor, from lung cancer!" I exclaimed. "Your story would give so many others hope, Mrs. Conch. We raised $25,000.00 on Saturday."

"I get tired of them asking for money all the time. Don't you? They always ask at the grocery store and they come to my door. I have no time," she responded, dismissing me.

I wanted to tell her she was fortunate enough to be enrolled in a screening trial for people who had been lifelong smokers and had quit, which is why her cancer was discovered at a stage where she not only had a choice of treatment options, she was cured of a cancer that is normally a death sentence by the time it's diagnosed. I had difficulty with the fact she had never once given back to the centre, not a moment of her time volunteering now that she was given an extension of her life, not a moment to help others to find hope as they embarked on their journey through cancer treatment, and not a penny to those who were working to find a cure. Fortunately, I kept my mouth shut. It seemed as though Karma or as Magnus would say, negativity, might be catching up with Mrs. Conch now.

"I'll do everything I can do," I tell her. "The cancer centre has some very good support groups organized by volunteers who have been through cancer treatment either themselves or with a spouse. That might help you both to better understand this time and to make some decisions."

"They already gave us that information at the centre," Mr. Conch tells me lowering his head and slowly shaking it from side to side.

"Is there nothing else you can offer?" she demands again.

"I'll have Carol review what we have for resources to make sure you have everything that's available to you," I tell them and pause for a moment before picking up my laptop and leaving the room.

It's a long day, but when it eventually ends, I realize how much easier my days have become since I started to understand the power of both positive and negative energy. Those that choose to be negative despite being warned, despite positive influence, despite an opportunity to change must be left to their own demise. There is far too much negativity in the world to be sucked down into it.

One must move on and stay positive for this is the only way to create more positive energy and to stay on one's path.

My Saturday morning begins with a call from Tom.

"Well, now I know why Josh wanted to meet with me," he begins. "I remember talking to him before he left for college about opportunists who look for someone to attach themselves to that has a better future than their own. He wanted me to meet his girlfriend; I think to give him my seal of approval."

"And?"

"Well I guess I can understand in a way why he's mesmerized by her. At first glance she looks pretty good, but remove the fake boobs, bleached hair, and add ten years to her and she'll start looking like the impostor she really is. She has absolutely no love in her heart for Josh, but it must look good for someone like her to be on the arm of a brilliant young ball player who has nothing but opportunity in his future."

"Oh no! I'm sorry to hear that, Tom. What now?"

"Well I'm meeting him Sunday before he leaves, just the two of us so I'll spend some time thinking about what to say to him when he asks what I think about her. I'm not looking forward to that part of the visit."

"Are they planning to get married or something?"

"They just started living together so the puppy is next on the horizon I guess."

"What does Josh's Mom think about all of this, Hunny? Do you know?"

"I'm planning to spend the day with my brothers tomorrow, Baby. We're going fishing."

"Well don't fall out of the boat! Better still, make sure you wear a life jacket okay?"

*"The aerial doesn't have many memories of the mother of Josh, Powerful One. You will know more in time. We tried to help the boy. I will be with you soon,"* and with that, the line goes dead. Magnus doesn't say good-bye as there really is no end with energy. It seemed unusual when I was first communicating with Magnus, but I've become accustomed to it now. I think for a moment about Tom avoiding questions about the woman he was with prior to me. He speaks openly about everything but her. It's as if he doesn't even hear me when I've asked or commented on Josh's Mom. As any woman would be, I'm very curious.

I head out on my road bike for an early morning ride after my call imagining Tom sitting across the table from Josh and his girlfriend, seeing through everything, hearing what they're not saying, and having to keep his comments to himself while they both try to convince him of their love for one another. I often worry about Tom seeing something from my past or something I'm thinking but not recognizing or not wanting to talk about. These are the things that Magnus has warned me about with Tom. Poor Tom I think as I rise off my saddle and grind up the last couple hundred meters of the hill before it flattens out along the orchard. Poor Josh I conclude as I sit back down and continue pedalling, recalling one particular conversation.

"The guy wants the sexy girlfriend with the bleach blond hair and the tramp stamp on her lower back and she wants the cool boyfriend with the barbed wire tattoo around his bicep and the 4x4 with the downhill bike in the back. They start dating and quickly become inseparable. She wants to have sex multiple times a day to show him how much she loves him and he thinks he's in seventh heaven, choosing blow jobs and getting laid over spending time with the guys. Then comes the time to get a puppy and move in together, showing everyone they're responsible and sealing the deal on a commitment," Tom told me as he pointed out a young couple along the trail that we were walking on at the time.

I noticed the attractive female with long blond hair and a nice figure, but she was completely ignoring her man and texting on her phone. He was walking along behind, holding the leash of a small lapdog that's sniffing and peeing, waiting with the poop bag. The look of disgust on his face as he tended to the dog was almost comical, but sad at the same time.

"Next comes the pressure to get married and start a family or maybe she gets pregnant," Tom continued. "Her interest in sex becomes less as she grows with the pregnancy, and his once attentive presence is lessened with her focus on the upcoming addition rather than him and his needs. He starts getting back in touch with his buddies and before long he's heading away with the boys on the weekends to ride his bike again, having a few pints in the pub during the week, and she starts to resent what she once liked about him, knowing there's plenty of sexy girls waiting to party with the boys like she once was. It's a recipe for disaster really."

"Not all relationships are like that are they?" I asked with disappointment in my voice.

"All that are based on materialistic things. He wants to have the best looking girl and she wants the popular guy so they convince themselves it's love. When blindness comes before love, nothing good comes of it."

I slide onto the end of a long train of riders as I head back toward the city, hoping that Josh can break away from the train he's on before it derails and crashes.

After a hot shower and breakfast, my cell phone rings. I'm delighted to hear from my childhood friend Sherry who's here for the weekend. We've always kept in touch, but it's been years since we've seen one another.

"What are you doing, Tesh? Can we get together? I'm here with a couple of girlfriends and we're going out tonight. You should come with us, it'll be just like old times!" she exclaims with excitement in her voice.

"I'd love to see you, Sherry. Can you and your friends come over for a glass of wine?" I ask.

She tells me she'll figure out what their plans are for the day and then let me know, and we eventually decide on them coming over for happy hour around 4pm. I spend the afternoon cleaning and shopping for wine and appetizers to serve the girls, recalling one of the last times I saw Sherry.

"I'm pretty much done with Jay. He's completely unmotivated to do anything. It's pathetic! I can't get him to mow the lawn or clean up the garage never mind help make dinner or clean up after himself even," she informed me.

Sherry and Jay were high school sweethearts, and one of the first to get married. Jay was one of those quieter boys who pretty much did what he was told when it came to Sherry. They struggled for years with infertility eventually having two girls. Sherry suffered with depression during those trying years and Jay was a pillar, reassuring her of his love for her at every turn. She gained an enormous amount of weight with the combination of antidepressant treatment and then fertility medications, but none of that seemed to matter to him. I was elated to see her so happy when the girls eventually came along, but she slowly started to turn her dissatisfaction toward her husband, always insisting that he pick up the pace. Jay was a doting father and delivered the girls to all of their activities, cheering them on as they danced and played sports, and cuddling up with them every night for hours of reading together. What he didn't do, however, was live up to Sherry's expectations in other areas of life, the yard work, the small jobs around the house, and keeping himself fit and youthful looking. Sherry, on the other hand, worked hard to lose weight, kept up appearances with her friends and wanted to be one of those active families while raising their girls. She hated that Jay enjoyed watching television and wasn't the least bit bothered by a messy house. I wondered now whether their relationship had weathered the storm.

Three dolled up women arrive on my doorstep just after 4pm on Saturday afternoon and my reunion with Sherry begins. She's dressed in slim fitting blue jeans that have an enormous amount of rhinestone bling along the front and rear pockets, a bright green loose fitting blouse, low cut in the front showing off the ample breasts she'd had since junior high, and black pumps with matching purse. Her hair is light blonde with streaks of brown that remind me of her natural colour when we were kids and I notice how nice her gel fingernails look with their French manicure polish. I can't help but notice she isn't wearing her ring on her left hand either.

Sherry's friends, Delilah and Johanna, are dressed similarly, tight jeans, pumps and tops that accentuate their breasts but are loose enough to hide the bellies that come with middle age. Johanna is sporting a set of store bought boobs that are so large on her petite frame it's hard not to stare. They are massive!

"You look great Tesh!" Sherry gushes as we pour wine and set out the food, sitting ourselves on the patio furniture on the deck.

"Thank you, Sherry, so do you. I'm glad you guys could come."

It's another half hour or so of small talk before we get into the meat and potatoes of female conversation. I confirm what Sherry has heard through the grapevine about no longer being with

# THE BEGINNING

Ken and we each briefly talk about our kids. I tell them I live with Tom, but don't say much more than that. It's easy to avoid speaking about my situation as the girls seem eager to talk about other things. Sherry has already been separated from Jay a couple of years now; he still isn't with anyone and according to Sherry is hanging on to hope that they might find their way back to one another. "Not in this lifetime!" she confirms. Johanna has a boyfriend that is a well-known celebrity from his history in politics. He's returned to his law practice and she thinks they're close to moving in together now. Delilah is the only one of the three who is married, but seems to be quite unsatisfied with her husband's inability to adequately provide for the family.

"We came for the Cattleman's conference," Sherry giggles and then continues, "you know, to see if we can get a good ride!"

"Sherry's new man is a rancher and we thought there might be some good fun to be had at the country bars this weekend," Delilah adds.

"We had fun last night, that's for sure!" Johanna cheers with her glass and finishes her wine with one large swallow.

"Oh, good to hear I live in a fun town," I add.

"You and Delilah were at U of C at the same time, Tesh," Sherry interjects. "I know it's a big campus and she was an art major, but Delilah's from there so maybe you know a few of the same people."

"I didn't get to know that many people when I was in University, but one of my friends in second and third year lived just off campus with her parents. Do you know Laurie Shore, Delilah?" I ask.

"Yes! I went to the same high school as Laurie, but she was a year older than me and her brother Adam was a year younger so I didn't know either of them personally," she replies and after a hesitation adds, "fortunately for me."

"We lost track of one another in fourth year and I don't even know if she went on to medical school. Why do you say fortunately for you, Delilah?" I enquire.

"I'm guessing you didn't hear her father was charged with sexual assault then?"

I gasp, thoughts rushing back about my experience as Delilah continues.

"Her parents used to have parties for both Laurie and her brother when they were in university and her Dad was apparently drugging people so he could have sex with them. They think he was putting something into drinks and giving his wife a sleeping pill. I think he was using date rape drug or something, I can't remember, but how they caught him was Adam's girlfriend thought she was having nightmares and then she turned up pregnant with

Dr. Shore's baby. The police found he'd been videotaping in Laurie's bathroom. It was a huge scandal at the time. He did time and he and his wife divorced of course. Laurie and Adam just sort of disappeared after that. I don't even think they live there anymore. Can you imagine your own Dad doing that?"

"I never heard anything about that," I add. "Poor Laurie, I can't imagine."

Everyone commented as I had. Trying to imagine how someone could do such a thing was difficult for anyone to fathom. I quickly wondered what would have happened if I had said something that night or the next morning. Would anything have changed because of it? I was relieved when the conversation changed back to the events of last night.

"We thought we'd see Sherry's boyfriend, but he didn't seem to want to hook up with us so we really pissed him off by having fun without him. Sherry knows another rancher, Cam the Cowboy, who's single and texted us saying they were heading to the Corral. When Mr. Married Pants found out he was some upset I'll tell ya!"

"Your boyfriend's married?" I ask Sherry.

"Yes, he's in a really unhappy relationship and is waiting for the last of the kids to leave home so he can get out of jail, too. But I told him I was going out to have some fun. I'm not married. I liked that he was acting possessive. I think it shows that he cares," she adds.

"Oh and he should be pissed knowing you're going out, just look at you. You're hot!" Delilah points at Sherry and holds her wine glass up to cheer.

"What he should have done was call Cam because they know one another and tell him to keep his grubby hands off!" Johanna states with authority.

The married man who's having an affair should call the single guy and tell him not to screw around with his piece of ass.... that makes a lot of sense I think, but keep my mouth shut instead of speaking my mind.

"It was fun learning how to two step and the boys at the western bar were great teachers. We dumped Cam and his friends eventually and went for a midnight ride in one of the guys ski boats, then partied until the wee hours in their hotel room. They were staying in a couple of suites at El Grande near the waterfront and we each got hooked up for some good ol' steer wrestling!" Sherry laughs as she recalls last night.

"I was with one of those guys that wanna fuck from behind, which I love especially when their dick is on the small side. Feels bigger that way, but it fuckin' fills me with air and I have those embarrassing cunt farts!" she laughs.

"I know!" exclaims Johanna. "It's impossible to keep those from coming out! Kerry loves that position, too, but when I start cunt farting I can't help laughing, and then he can't cum."

"Well I wasn't doin' any cunt farting last night. I'm the only one that didn't get ridden by a bull last night," Delilah adds. "But I must say I sure had him excited," she giggles, hiding her mouth with her hand. "I might just have to find a better specimen tonight."

"Until Kerry puts a ring on my finger I'm gonna have fun," Johanna says placing her hands beneath her breasts gently lifting and moving them from side to side. "That's what these babies are for!" she laughs.

"I'm lookin' for the man in the suit who can provide and still knows how to fix the dishwasher when it breaks down," Sherry adds. "I have to have a man in a suit, there's just no getting around that. Jay wore a suit and made good money in the end, but he just wouldn't do a bloody thing around the place. He'd rather read a book or watch TV than visit with people. Drove me nuts."

"He was always reading in high school, sounds like that hasn't changed," I say. He was good enough when you were depressed and fat, but now he's pathetic, I think to myself, empathizing with Jay.

"No, he wouldn't change, that was the problem. I really started resenting that about him. When he told me to go ahead and hire a regular cleaning lady and call the plumber to fix the dishwasher, I lost it. I knew we were done then and there," Sherry states. "You've gotta come out with us tonight, Tesh. We used to have so much fun in high school, dancing and getting drunk. Remember? The boys always flocked around you then and you're every bit as sexy to look at now!" she pleads.

"Oh do tell!" Johanna says leaning forward on her chair.

"Come on, Sherry. We could use a good story or two from your high school days," adds Delilah.

"Well because we grew up in a smaller town, and there was lots of countryside around, our parties were generally outside. Usually there was a bonfire and it was often near the river or at the lake. When there was water around that usually meant people were taking their clothes off to go swimming. I remember going to one of those parties with Bev Harper and all the guys went skinny dipping. Ben Douglas was yelling at me from in the water calling me chicken and taunting me to take off my clothes and come in. I not only stripped and jumped in, I also fucked Ben in the bush that night, too," she throws her head back and laughs. "Do you remember that, Tesh?"

"Yes, I was done with him by then," I add, pretending to yawn.

"Good thing. He fucked *really* hard. He took me from behind and was pulling my hair and ramming his cock inside me. It fuckin' hurt! He even slapped me on the ass a couple of times and at the end he didn't even say anything. Oh well, I guess I just wanted to get fucked too anyhow. Ben was Tesh's first," Sherry informs the others. "That's when Tessy was a cowboy herself," she says laughing. "Riding her horse to Ben's every day and getting fucked while the rest of us were still playing with our Barbie dolls and having Ken and Barbie live out our fantasies!" she continues as we all laugh.

"Do you remember when their Dad died? Wasn't that horrible? He was crushed wasn't he, Tessy?"

"He was on a hillside in a tractor that didn't have a cab. It tipped and rolled over him. He was barely alive when they found him seven or eight hours later. They say he must have suffered like a fox in a leg hold trap. He died in hospital that night." I say without emotion and when the girls moan I wonder if I'm becoming hardened from my years as a doctor.

"And then there was the time that we all watched Mattress Myrna get gang banged in the back of Kevin Long's car," Sherry changes the subject and continues, recalling more of the sexual experiences of our youth. "All you could see besides her legs in the air was a white bum going up and down in the back seat, and everyone was having a look through the windows that's for sure," she describes as she stands and moves her bum back and forth. "That was the same night that ugly Ernie had a turn I think. The next week at school everyone, including Myrna herself, was saying she did it for her country." Sherry has us all in stitches.

"Ok don't say anything more until I pee!" Delilah cries as both she and Sherry jump up to use the washroom and Johanna heads for a fresh bottle of wine.

I feel a pang of unease and anxiety as I recall the summer when I turned thirteen and my almost daily visits to the wood shed. Lying on the couch while Ben shoved his cock inside me and shot his load with barely any touching of each other's bodies. He'd even stopped kissing me after the second or third time together. I remember the anticipation of the visit exciting me and making me tingle between my legs, but the abruptness of the experience was disappointing and frustrating. I didn't know what I could do about it, but I knew I wanted more. It wasn't until I became confident while giving Daren a blow job that I actually remember enjoying sex or what I believed to be sex. I don't know why I stopped going back. My desire was stronger after each visit, and yet I'd stopped going. Maybe that's when my period started and I knew I had to be careful. I guess that's why I stopped seeing Ben. I remember being with Daren after that summer when I was getting rides from school, but never back at their place. The next couple of years until I was on the pill were spent giving blow jobs and having boyfriends where I used a condom, but my memories from then are fragmented for some reason.

Sherry and Delilah return from the washroom and Johanna finishes refilling our wine glasses, interrupting my thoughts with laughter and the beginning of more story telling.

"The best summer was when Tessy got her license and car!" Sherry starts. "Freedom! We went to the drive-in every Friday night during the summer and I don't think we ever saw a movie. There was either a dance or a bush party on Saturday night. Do you remember the time we went fucking camping, Tessy? You got some real good looking guy to come over and help us set up our tents. Afterward we drew straws to see who would go over and give him a blow job and I lost."

"No. You won. I'd have done it without even drawing straws, but we had to be fair."

"Ya, so I go over and offer him head and he turns me down! Turns out he was gay!" Sherry roars with laughter. "We had the best weekend with those boys. He had three friends show up later and it was like partying with four more girls!"

"My stomach hurts! I haven't laughed this much for ever!"

"Me either. My makeup must be halfway down my face."

"My little red Volkswagen had some busy nights back then that's for sure," I add. "Do you remember helping me climb over the fence at the Ventners so I could sneak in the window and screw? I wasn't dating little dink Greg any more, but I could count on him in a pinch," I add. "He always wanted to put it in my bum. I didn't want it in my bum!"

"Kept me from getting pregnant," Johanna says thoughtfully. "I grew to really like anal sex actually. As long as you're doing it with someone you can trust not to just shove it in there before you're ready. That and giving hand jobs. I gave a lot of hand jobs in high school."

"One of the girls in my building has only done it the cunt to get pregnant," adds Sherry. "She can't cum unless it's in her ass."

"Seriously!" I've only tried it a couple times. I don't really like it. It makes me feel like I have to have a shit!" Delilah laughs. "I don't like giving hand jobs either. Too messy when they cum all over my hand. I don't even like giving blow jobs. Too much work, and I choke. There's no fuckin' way I would swallow that either! Inside me is best, then I can flush it."

"That's the best part," I say. "After working for it, there's no way I'm wasting it. I get excited when I know it's getting close, their breathing gets quicker and they lie still concentrating on getting there. It's wonderful. My mouth starts to water," I add and find myself getting excited just thinking of it.

"You don't have to put it all the way in your mouth. I only put my mouth on the end and use my hand to go up and down. That way I don't choke and my hand does most of the work," Sherry says. "My cowboy doesn't seem to want me blowin' him as much as he likes putting it in my ass. Once I let him know I was game, he wants to do it that way all the time now. I'm good with it," Sherry shrugs and continues. "I'm pretty happy with this one actually. I see him at least once a month and we fuck all weekend. I need a break after that!"

"I get it every couple weeks at home," Delilah adds. "That's enough for me!"

"Kerry's pretty horny still so we fuck a lot. Every time we're together so a couple times a week I guess." Johanna concludes.

I don't think they'd believe me if I told them I'd been having sex twice a day since Tom and I had been living together, and am finding it almost unbearable being without him and that lovely dick of his this past week. I keep my mouth shut and Sherry changes the subject.

"It's a wonder more kids didn't get knocked up in high school actually, but I guess lots of the girls were on the pill then. We didn't use condoms as much as we should have I know that, but there really wasn't the same diseases to worry about then or maybe it was because we were in a small community. People were clean."

"I think it's where you grew up. My girlfriend screwed a lot of guys when she was young and she had many many appointments to get warts burned off inside her cunt she had so many," Johanna adds and sends a shiver through each of us. "I was horny in high school, but nothing like what I've been since my divorce. I think those years of marriage were so awful that I'm still trying to make up for it. I screwed two different guys in one day even. Well the teacher I gave a blow job to and the carpenter I screwed, but there were two in one day. I was blowing the teacher in the kitchen and he finally had to finish it off and shot it all over the place. I don't swallow either, Delilah. He was so embarrassed while he was cleaning it up and I just stood there watching him and pointing at places where there was cum. Some of it even landed on my shoe. It was pretty funny actually. Those weren't my proudest moments, but I think I really just needed to let loose."

"We all want to let loose sometimes, Hunny. And that's why we're here!" concludes Sherry.

"Imagine what it's like now with everyone having smart phones and taking pictures at parties. I shudder to think of what it might have been like if Myrna had seen herself on Facebook the next day after being with all those guys in Kevin's car. Then it was no big deal really, but today I think people are looking for opportunities to post something. Maybe they're not looking for opportunities, but don't realize what could happen if they did. We just laughed about it and it was forgotten the next weekend when Danny the drunk passed out naked at the lake and everyone saw his pecker, but it's pretty hard to forget something that's gone viral," I add.

"I think kids are worse now. It's just that much easier to be a cyber-bully so they do it. Or they have a fight with someone and then post a really nasty picture of them to hurt them back," Delilah says as she finishes her glass of wine. "I'm so glad I'm not a teenager these days that's all I know."

"Would you have texted Jay a picture of me giving the guy we picked up hitch hiking a blow job in the back seat of your VW if we had had an argument, Tessy?" Sherry enquires.

"Never, but I sure as hell would have threatened!" we both laugh, neither of us wanting to take the conversation too seriously, knowing our days in high school would have been very different today.

I start to notice each of them glancing at their phones, counting down the hours before the night of fun begins. When one of the men from last night text, they decide they should head out to have dinner before meeting them at another of the local western bars, this time the one with the mechanical bull. Looks like the girls are all gonna get a ride tonight, and I don't mean a ride in the taxi cab either!

As I say good-bye and give Sherry an extra hug while the other two head for the taxi, she whispers in my ear.

"Oh how I wish you were coming with us, Tesh. The men Johanna attracts are not the kind that want to settle down with someone and that's what I'm really after now."

As they drive away and we wave at one another, I say out loud what's in my head, "Neither are the ones you're attracting at that place my friend."


Tom calls as I'm getting ready for bed and we talk about his day of fishing with his brothers. He relates how they spent the day talking about times spent in their fishing boat as kids. He tells me it was every bit as fun today as it had been all those years ago, but he hopes they're all wiser now than what they were in those days.

"Did I ever tell you about the time my sister and I nearly drown?" he asks.

"Tom! That's not really what I want to hear right now."

"I'm sorry, but it's kind of a good story actually. My sister Ruth and I took the row boat out one Saturday morning and we thought we'd row out to the end of the pier and back. The wind came up and it started to get choppy so we decided to turn around and come back. As we were making our turn, a wave clipped us and put the boat over. I was thrown away from the boat and when I came to the surface the chop was getting bigger and I couldn't get back to the boat. I could hear Ruth calling for me, but I wasn't strong enough to get to the overturned boat. Ruth was hanging on and I was about to go under for the last time when I felt someone grab me by the collar. He lifted me into his boat, pulled alongside our boat to rescue Ruth from the water and then towed our boat into shore. He seemed to have appeared out of nowhere. Ruth and I huddled together on the bench seat, teeth chattering, and I remember him smoking his pipe with one hand and steering his boat with the other as he brought us in. He silently lifted us out of his boat one at a time. He pulled our boat up onto the sandy shoreline and then nodded toward us as he pushed his boat back out and jumped aboard. It wasn't until he was disappearing on the water that we thought to wave and yell thank you. And it was years later before either of us spoke of how lucky we were that day.

"Awe Jeez, Tom. Thank goodness for that."

"I'll tell you about the other time I nearly drowned another day, Baby. Don't wanna upset ya too much. How was your day?"

I describe my bike ride and then my visit with Sherry, Delilah and Johanna, relating much of our conversation. "I feel very badly for Sherry's husband. All he did was fail to live up to someone's expectations and for that he and his love were cast aside."

"That's right. The young couple get together out of physical attraction and then do things in bed, having sex more than they'd ever really care to, only to hook the other. They get the animal to show they're responsible. Then they have a child and soon stop having sex. All of a sudden they say they're no longer in love and they're getting a divorce, but love was never part of the equation in the first place. They love the dog. They love their job. They love their apartment. They have no idea what love means. It starts earlier because we teach our kids the wrong meaning of love and they sometimes wonder if a parent loves their sibling more than them because they don't really have a grasp of what love is. Parents don't openly demonstrate love towards each other unless friends are over and then there's a bit more show of happiness in the relationship, but it's generally one of raising kids, paying bills, collecting stuff and so on. These women are no different; they're out screwing men, hoping to land something that has what they want, in this case money. But what they don't realize is they're now 15 or 20 years older and not that appealing any longer. What they are is cleaner than hookers on the street. These men go to these places to find a dumping station, not a wife. They already have a wife at home so they're happy when they find a divorcee or a married woman because those women fuck harder than they ever would with their husbands. It doesn't cost them that much and is a helluva lot safer. So just because she might find someone who wears a suit and makes good money, there's nothing saying he's gonna want to fix the dishwasher. Just because he can doesn't mean he will. His job is wearing the suit and making money, he doesn't see his job as fixing the dishwasher. This guy already has a cleaning lady and someone to do yard maintenance so if the dishwasher breaks, he calls the plumber. He doesn't want to share that part of his life with her. When he's not working, he wants to go out, get on his boat and relax with his kids and his phoney trophy wife that tries to speak with a foreign accent. He does want to fuck one of these, but that's as far as he wants to go. That's what these ladies can't seem to comprehend. The men are the same. The income tax bracket changes, that's all. She can screw him in his suit and tell him she likes it in her bum and give him blow jobs every day, but he will never want to be with her. Do you think that man is going to walk away from a beautiful home in a prestigious neighbourhood, his Lexus, his Mastercraft wake boat, and his vacation home on the lake for one of those women? These guys are not stupid, that's how they got where they are. Baby I hate to say this, but you more than anyone should know what greed is about. All these people do today is try to see whose debt makes them look the best. They'll live with someone they don't love just to keep their stuff. You might think they're unhappy but they're not because they have their stuff. People will choose boats and homes and cars over love.

"I know. It just saddens me to see my friends like this, that's all. I wish they could hear what you're saying and understand what I now know."

"*They will never understand my Powerful One. Everyone is given chances, but most choose the negative side and not the positive. They want what they cannot have and will give up what they have to get it. They have lost their path and will find it difficult to find it.*"

"Magnus, I'm so glad to hear your voice. I've had many memories stirred up by the girls visit and the old photos I've been looking through. I'm worried Tom might see something before I can speak these things to you. Please, I don't want to make any mistakes," I beg.

"*Relax my Powerful One. I'll be sending an energy to help guide you on your path.*"

"What do you mean?"

"*What I mean is what I spoke. Relax. I will be with you soon.*"

And with those words, the conversation ends and the line goes dead.

# CHAPTER 9
## Moving Forward

I tell myself there's nothing to worry about and am about to turn out the lights when a text message comes in from Ken.

> I have to work Sun. Can you take girls?

> Yes of course

> I'll drop them at 11 pick up 6ish

I start my morning earlier than usual with a bike ride then head to the grocery store to get some things for a picnic. I quickly shower and am finishing packing our lunch as the girls arrive.

# THE BEGINNING

"Hi Mom. We're here!" Bella yells as they walk in dropping their back packs on the floor at the entrance.

"Hello! " I respond, walking open armed toward the entrance, and hug both girls at once.

"We brought our butterfly nets and bug cages, Mom. Look!" Juliette squeals, holding her new bug cage in the air to show me.

"Can we catch some butterflies today?" Bella asks excitedly.

"We'll take them on our walk. Where do your backpacks go?" I remind the girls of their responsibility with their belongings. "Have you had breakfast?"

"Yup, we're not hungry," Bella calls behind her as they quickly hang their packs on the coat stand and head for their bedroom.

After a few minutes getting reacquainted with their room and the cat, we head out in the car.

"Can we have sushi for lunch?" Juliette asks.

"No burgers!" Bella adds.

"I didn't pack sushi or burgers."

"No wait, let's go to Joe's! They have the best desserts there."

"Ya, I want a milkshake."

"You're not allowed. You didn't eat your dinner last time remember?"

"Tattle tale!"

I'm quickly reminded of what my girls are becoming as they squabble in the back seat behind me, and I begin to recall how Tom had gently pointed out I was responsible for feeding their greed in the beginning too. I always seemed to have a "little something" for them when we'd start our two weeks together after my separation from Ken. Tom asked me to watch closely on their day of arrival and I was shocked to witness what I had been oblivious to until it was pointed out to me. The girls came running into the town-house and before saying anything ran to their bedroom to see what was waiting on their beds and then quickly looked at each other's to make sure they got the same. They were more excited to see what they were getting than to see their Mom. They didn't even acknowledge Tom.

I started to see my girls differently and took notice of how they'd expect to have something bought for them each time we were in a store, and it wasn't necessarily candy or a toy. They asked for things they didn't even want just to see if they could get me to buy it for them. One day during a big grocery shop, Bella and Juliette each put a Christmas ornament in the shopping cart. I took them out when they weren't looking and the ornaments were never mentioned again, not when we arrived home and unpacked groceries and not when we decorated the Christmas tree.

Ken and I had an argument because he wanted to buy each of the girls a cell phone for Christmas last year and expected I would agree to pay for half. I said absolutely not and argued that 10 year olds shouldn't have cell phones and would get into trouble with ones that allowed them to surf on the internet. When the girls arrived at my house on Christmas Day they seemed subdued.

"I got this hat and my purse," Bella said.

"I got that too and some Lego and we each got a movie," Juliette added.

"I didn't think your Dad would buy you purses!"

"He didn't, that was from Auntie."

"Well what did Daddy get you then?"

"I don't remember," Bella answered as Juliette walked out of the room.

"I think you would remember what your Dad bought you for Christmas, Hunny." I said to Bella. "Juliette, come back here please. What's going on?" I asked. "What's wrong?"

"Dad told us not to tell you we got phones for Christmas. We weren't allowed to bring them because he said you'd take them away and not give them back again," Bella admitted. And that was one of the many examples of his not only coaching the girls to lie to me, but of his buying their love with material purchases.

"Mom! Are we having lunch?" Bella asks.

"We sure are."

"But you just passed Joe's." Juliette whines.

"I have picnic lunch for our walk today. When were you guys at Joe's anyway?"

"Lots of times!" Juliette continues. "That's why we like it there."

"They're always happy to see us when we come in. Why can't we go?"

"You'll enjoy this more than Joe's. Just wait and see."

We hike along the creek and enjoy a picturesque afternoon, spotting deer and eagles along the way. When Juliette starts to ask the time every few minutes, I know she's counting down the moments until they can return to wonderland. As we're driving past the golf course on our way home from our hike, Juliette spots her Dad's truck.

"There's Daddy's truck! They're still golfing."

"Oh I see Nanny and Poppy's car beside the truck," Bella adds excitedly.

"I thought Daddy had to work today. I didn't know he was golfing."

"No he's not working. We went out for dinner with Nanny and Poppy to celebrate cause Sandy sold a house and they all decided to go golfing today. That's why we had to come to your house, Mom."

"There they are!" Bella yells, spotting them making their way back to the clubhouse.

"Awesome! Do you want me to drop you here, girls?"

"Yes!" They both yell in unison.

"Daddy will be so surprised!" Juliette exclaims and claps her hands together.

"You bet he will," I say as I turn into the driveway of the golf course and pull up under the canopy at the front entrance. I barely have the car stopped before the girls have their seat belts off and are scrambling to get going.

"I want to tell Daddy. I saw them first!"

"So!"

"Bye girls. "Love you!"

"Love you too, Mom," Bella yells as she slams the car door.

"Bye Mom. I love you," Juliette calls out as she turns to run and catch her sister.

Neither thanks me as is the norm. When Tom mentioned one day that kids need to learn when to say thank you on their own I stopped reminding the girls to be polite and say thank you. Telling them doesn't teach them to be thankful; it only teaches them when to say two words. Just as telling a child to say sorry doesn't mean they will understand why they're saying it, it only means they will learn how to back out of what they've done unless it's explained properly and then left up to them to learn when to say it. I was still waiting for them to appreciate and be grateful for the efforts of others, and it seemed I'd be waiting a long time. I drive away with a smile on my face, however, knowing that Ken's plans for cocktails after golf with the adults had just become a family affair.

I return home and enjoy a hot shower, cold beer and then curl up on the love seat with Rex to start reading *Calm* by Mary Katherine Fontanero, the third of a four book series that Tom gave me for my forty-fifth birthday.

Monday mornings vary for me. Sometimes I have a shift at the walk-in clinic, other times I schedule longer appointments in my office or catch up on admin, and once a month I take an entire day off. This Monday is a four hour shift in the walk-in clinic, which I'm thankful for as time will fly by until it's time to meet Tom at the airport.

The walk-in clinic shifts are challenging as the patients and problems are very diverse, but I've learned over the years to accept that I can't solve everyone's problem in one ten minute visit and often can only provide a band aid to get them through their trials and tribulations. Often my own patients track me down at the clinic which seems to be the case this morning when I see Judy is my first patient. I smell alcohol as soon as I walk into the room and see a dishevelled Judy who starts speaking immediately.

"I just can't cope with this any longer. He's being completely fucking unreasonable about this. I didn't do anything to that fucker. I gave and gave and did everything I could for that man! My income has paid for everything," Judy yells as she stands up and starts to pace in the examining room.

"Are you saying Rod wasn't working?" I ask already knowing the answer.

"Oh yes he's working, but not nearly as hard as me and not making the kind of money I'm fucking making. I can't fucking believe it. I can't stay with them anymore and I can't go back home. Chuck said he has to go home because that cunt is upset and he's worried about the kids now. How about my fucking kids?! Is she thinking about them?! I don't fucking think so! What about my fucking needs? It's all about her and her fucking kids! Well fuck them! Fuck all of them!" Judy yells staggers and sits back down.

"I need you to calm down now, Judy. We're in the walk-in clinic and it's difficult for me to help you here, but I can help you if you allow me to," I say as calmly and with as much reassurance in my voice as I'm able to convey.

"Yes, I need help. I know I need help," Judy confirms and starts to cry. "I haven't slept for days Dr. Peterson," she sobs.

"Let's take care of this right now, Judy. I'm going to call an ambulance," I tell her as she nods her head and cries uncontrollably.

When I open the door to speak with the receptionist, I see the RCMP officers coming through the door, and hear the faint sound of a siren which I assume is the ambulance.

"Are you okay? I called when I heard her start to yell, Dr. Peterson."

"Thank you. Yes. I think she'll come out on her own. Give me a minute," I say as I return to the room.

"The ambulance is almost here, Judy. Just relax now. Everything is okay."

Judy continues to cry, and is too weak to resist the ambulance attendants, the stretcher or the ambulance ride to the hospital. When the receptionist interrupts another appointment for me to take a call from the psychiatric team lead later that morning, I tell them what I know of Judy's situation and my assessment of her now.

By the time my shift at the clinic is over, I feel like I've worked a full eight hour shift, not four, but once showered and on my way to the airport, I feel like a new woman! I park the car and rush into the terminal, locating an arrivals monitor and anxiously looking for Tom's flight. I feel a sense of relief when I finally find what I'm looking for and see his flight is on time, only ten more minutes to wait. I can neither sit nor stand so I decide to use the washroom and when I return to the monitor, I see his flight has now been updated to "Arrived". My heart is pounding as I wait to see him walking on the other side of the glass corridor before coming through the doors. I've never felt anything like this before. Ken and I would be apart for longer periods and more often and I had never felt this kind of yearning, excitement, anxiety or any of the emotions I was feeling at this very moment as I anticipate seeing Tom again. It is as if I can feel his presence in the terminal now and I'm almost beside myself with love for this man. I silently vow to never let him out of my sight. Nothing is worth us being apart for this long again. I see him through the glass barrier as he walks down the ramp toward the arrivals area. I feel my heart pounding in my chest, my ears become silent to the noise of the terminal and everything seems to slow down. I feel as if I'm in a Guy Ritchie movie as the scene in front of me slowly unfolds. Tom turns his head and his eyes search for me. His eye brows raise and his expression becomes a smile as we make eye contact. He raises his hand to wave as he continues walking along the ramp. As he turns to face me and walks through the now opened doors, his arms extend outward to engulf me. At the moment we embrace, the special effects come to an end and I start to speak

"Oh Tom, I hated this! I missed you so much!"

"I hated it more and I missed you more. That will never change," he replies calmly.

Waiting for his luggage is excruciating as I can only think of kissing him passionately, burying my face in his chest and inhaling his scent. I am close to tears as we finally reach the car and embrace again. I want to call for Magnus, but am nervous as we've never been apart this long and I wonder if it might not be wise to try to connect with all these people around. I want to get home as quickly as possible and I hardly speak during the short drive to the town-house, unable to take my eyes off Tom as he drives, unable to focus on anything. I'm desperate to speak with the energy, to be reassured by Magnus that I am still on my path, that Tom hasn't felt something while he was away, and that I haven't made a mistake. Waiting to hear the voice is as painful as waiting for Tom to appear before me at the airport.

"Everything okay Baby?" Tom asks.

"I think so. I just love you so much, Tom. I'm feeling overwhelmed with emotion. I have a lump in my throat and an ache deep inside of me that I thought would leave as soon as we were together again, but it's still there."

"We'll be home soon and then everything will be fine, Baby, I promise."

"I could never survive without you, Tom."

We embrace for a long time once inside our home and I whisper in Tom's ear as I always do when I call for Magnus.

"I love you. I love you. I love you," and then I hear what I've been aching for.

"*And I am loving you my Powerful One. Relax now. I will be with you soon.*"

It is as if I've been holding my breath and can finally breathe again. Rex's sudden appearance and her incessant meowing for Tom is an interruption and the voice is gone. I move away from Tom so he can give Rex a quick tug of her ear as she leans her head toward him. It seems an odd thing for a cat to want, but Rex isn't exactly your typical feline. Tom walks into the kitchen, whistles at how clean it is and then quickly opens the pantry door pretending to uncover where the take-out food boxes might be hiding. Fortunately, I'd thought of that this morning before work, and pretend to be shocked by his accusations.

"You think I don't cook when you're not here?!"

"What exactly did you eat?" he asks, "opening the fridge door to show me there isn't much more than cream, wine and beer in there, and we both laugh.

"Well it's a good job food isn't on my mind right now," he comments, cracking open a beer then pouring the last of the wine into a glass for me. We walk outside onto the patio, sit close together on the love seat and start talking about Tom's trip.

"How was everyone in your family, Tom?"

"Funerals are a good way to see everyone that's for sure, and they all seemed good. I don't think Dad would even know she was gone. He's not looking good either now so it won't be long before I'll be making another trip.

"Not without me next time," I add.

"I know, Baby," and he squeezes my leg.

"I had a really good visit with the boys when we went fishing. They're as crazy as ever. Billy's line never hit the water. He just sat on the chair drinkin' beer and never shut his mouth."

I laugh as Tom talks about his brothers mimicking them and their accents.

"Jerry's maintenance on the boat was as bad as it always was, the bilge pump was running the whole time we were out. It could barely keep up with the water coming in."

*"Ya', I gotta get at that."* Jerry would say about the leaks.

*"Jerry said the same thing two years ago. He was gonna throw some paint on this ol' scowl. I see that got done!"* Billy would say.

*"She may be an old scowl, but that doesn't stop yer fat ass from bein' on it every time she leaves the harbor!"*

*"Well somebody's gotta go to help ya' dock this tub. It's costin' ya' far too much money repairin' docks. Remember that time ya' forgot to untie the bow line and we nearly took the dock off fishin' with us?"*

*"That was yer job Billy! I'm the captain. Yer the skiffy, remember?"*

*"I'll skiffy ya' one! But none the less ya' shoulda seen the look on everybody's face when we started yankin' that dock out!"*

*"It weren't that bad, Billy!"*

*"Well, it ruined that day o' fishin. Spent it nailin' that dock back together instead."*

*"Like you were gonna be doin' that. Still got yer quota of Moosehead in. I don't know what yer cryin' about."*

"Are you going to put your line in, Billy?" Bobby'd ask.

*"He ain't put bait on that thing in four years, why would he start now."*

"They were so funny, Baby. Bobby and I laughed at those two all day long. I think Bobby might buy the old homestead. Even though he doesn't live there anymore, he wants to hang on to the property. I don't really know why, but he's got the extra money I guess so that's what he wants to do," Tom continues and mimics his brothers conversation again.

*"Well , if you're buyin' the place, why don't ya' let me keep some of my stuff out there then, Bobby."*

*"Yup, then you'd have two junk piles ya' ol' coot!"*

"No Jerry I'd be renting the place out."

*"Well if ya' let me keep some things there, I can take care of the place for ya'."*

*"Oh now there's a good idea, havin' Jerry maintain yer place."*

"And they went on like that the entire time I was with them," he says as he takes a swig of his beer and glances at his watch. "Why don't we do dinner a la Tesh tonight and get it in a box."

"The old apple doesn't fall far from the tree," I kid back and pick up my cell phone." I happen to have a few local establishments in my contacts. You prefer pizza I assume?"

"Sounds good. We'll shop tomorrow," Tom replies, reaching for my phone and within a few moments is ordering our dinner.

"Yes I'd like to order a large pizza for delivery please. Yes, that's right, for Dr. Peterson. Yes that's the correct address. What did we order last time? I see. Yes, sounds good, but make it a *large*, not a *small*," Tom says, emphasizing the size of the pizza in the conversation. "Thank you. Okay. Yes, bring the debit machine. Bye now," and with that he hangs up. "Sounds like a nice pizza. I don't think I've ever had that before."

"Ok, ok. I knew I should have done the phoning. I'll not live that one down will I?"

"I'm gonna grab another beer. I'll bring in some plates and cutlery. How's your wine?"

"I'm good. I'll have a beer with you when the pizza comes," and it arrives a few minutes later as the daylight is just starting to fade.

"So tell me, Baby, how was your day?"

"It was good. I had a nice run first thing this morning. Today was my walk-in clinic shift and it was super busy, crazy actually. I think it had a lot to do with that," I say, pointing at the full moon that had just started to become visible on the horizon.

"What did you see?"

"I had a patient from my practice come to the walk-in this morning. I'm not sure if she knew I'd be there or she just needed to see someone, but I'm very glad she saw me because I was anticipating this downward spiral. She's so disconnected from her former self and absolutely oblivious to her part in her current problems. As soon as she came into reception, the girls put her in to a room, and Jan actually called 911 after hearing her ranting while we were in the examining room. The girls are both really good at anticipating problems that's for sure." I stop talking to take a drink of beer and then continue. "The attendants even commented how busy they've been the last couple of days and attribute it to this full moon. One good thing about the busy shift was it was done before I knew it and I was that much closer to getting ready to come and meet you at the airport," I gush and lean in to give Tom a kiss.

"How did things go on Sunday with Josh?"

"It went well. We had breakfast together and we talked about a few things as I thought. He said how they love each other and how much fun they have together. They've already got the dog! I told him the big thing is to take your time. You've got a promising career with baseball potentially and your education is important." Tom hesitates for a moment, then continues. "But I did tell him a story about one of the guys I worked with one time. His name was Fred and he told me how much he loved his girlfriend so I asked him what love was. He couldn't explain it to me. He said they were in love but was challenged to actually describe what love was. So I said you told me you loved your job, Fred. Well I like my job he replied. You said you loved the new hoist in the shop, Fred. And he said well ya it's a great hoist compared to the old one. You said you love hanging out with us guys from work. Well ya' I love working with you guys and I really do like hanging out with you guys, too. You see, that's the problem. We use the word love for everything and many don't know what love actually means. Loving someone means you love absolutely everything about them. You love them whether they're angry or bitchy or happy. You love them when they look beautiful, but also when they're not looking so good or have gained a few pounds. You love their good habits as well as their bad ones. You want to be together every minute of the day, not just when it's convenient to be together or when you're not with the guys from work. There is no ball and chain when you love someone. You like to make decisions, Fred. In a loving relationship you can't just make all the decisions unilaterally. You make all your decisions together with the person you love. You want them to be a part of all your decisions as a couple. There is no boss. It's equal and you want it to be equal because you love them. I asked Fred if he remembered when he bought the convertible, and she was so pissed because he didn't ask her about it? They didn't make that decision together. Just think of when you're working one day I said to Josh and maybe she's still in school. If you want a flat screen TV, do you just go and buy it because you make the money? Of course not because that's not right. It doesn't matter who makes the money in the relationship. Those are decisions you make together because you plan together, each having equal decision making power and that often means compromising. Love should not be measured on the way things look or on what you have. You told me you two were like best friends. Best friends? Love isn't about being "best friends" either. That's not correct. Best friends are more like brother and sister. A happy couple isn't best friends, they're a loving happy couple enjoying every moment, every inch of one another. Those brother sister relationships are the couples that look like one another. Their expressions are the same, and they start to dress the same. If one limps the other limps. That's a brother sister couple, and they may love one another, but not in the way a loving couple should. Take Tessy and I for example, we laugh, joke around all the time and maybe even make fun of people the odd time, but we never lose focus on who we are as individuals. We strive to make each other stronger, to support one another as individuals in a relationship. The stronger Tesh is, the stronger we are as a couple. And we don't look alike. Actually I think she's getting younger. I'm just getting bigger! Especially after being here with the brothers drinking all that Moosehead! Anyway I hope I got some things through to him."

As Tom speaks, I can't help but think back to my relationship with Ken. I had no decision making power and he rarely if ever asked my opinion on anything. Things were bought left right and centre. When I did have an opinion about something he'd already purchased, he'd get upset and tell me he'd take it back then! This was always done in a way that made me feel as though I'd just rained on his parade and it made me feel guilty when he'd done something for "us" as he'd say in his argument to me. I even was made to feel guilty when it was something he did solely for himself such as his golf membership at the most expensive golf course in the city. "I thought it would be nice for us to have dinner there and then for the girls to have lessons there one day. It's for the business and that is for us", he told me. Things are so different in my relationship with Tom.

"I'm sure you did reach him, Tom. He wanted to meet with you remember? He respects your opinion."

"Yup, who knows, it's entirely up to him. You can tell them, but you can't live their lives for them," Tom summarizes as he stands up to clean up our dinner dishes.

"Thanks for dinner Hunny. Where do you hide these or I mean keep these boxes?" he teases.

"Haw, Haw. They don't accept pizza boxes in the recycling so straight to the garbage," I reply as I pick up the remaining items from dinner, follow Tom into the kitchen, dropping my load on the counter, and taking my place on one of the bar stools. I sense something is different, but I can't quite put my finger on it. I chalk it up to our being apart for the past week, but for some reason I'm starting to feel a little bit uneasy. As Tom finishes loading the dishes into the vault as he calls it, grabs another beer from the fridge and sits on the seat beside me at the counter, he looks at me differently, as if assessing me.

# THE BEGINNING

"Well that's witch burn for sure," he speaks with a very clear tone and I know it isn't Tom or Magnus speaking. He appears to be looking at my hair. "Stand up then and let's have a look at you," he directs rather arrogantly. I stand as he instructs. "I thought energy doesn't see," I say wondering who I'm speaking to. "What do you mean witch burn? Are you referring to my hair?"

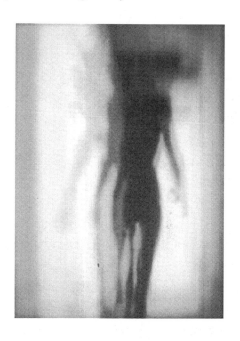

"Of course I'm referring to your hair. What else would I mean? Those white streaks through your hair are witch burn. Surprising really, you've shown no sign of it," he says in a dismissive tone.

"Sign of it? Are you saying I'm a witch?"

"Indeed you're a witch. You were a witch of sorts at one time, but it doesn't look like too much of that trait has come over. You dealt mainly with herbs and healing, and that is what you do now isn't it? Healing?

"Yes, I'm a doctor."

"But then, you dabbled a bit in the black arts as they called it, which eventually got you burnt. You are correct, energy cannot see in the same way you do. When he looks at you and feels joy and happiness, we get that feeling. When he sees or experiences something like being on a roller coaster, for example, and you're about to plummet downward, that feeling of fear that goes through him is what we feel. You've been with Magnus correct?"

"Yes."

"He's caressed you, held you, touched your breasts, so I know you're rather short, no tits, and so forth. This is all shared between the energies.

"Shared?"

"Yes, shared between all the energies. This is what keeps them positive, but we'll talk more about this, and the witch thing, but this time I'll be in charge so you shouldn't end up getting burnt."

"So if you already know what I look like, why did you ask me to stand?"

"To see how well you obey is all. Not that I care about what you look like anyway. I'm not really interested in you at all actually, but I've been sent here to babysit you. I don't know how you've gotten this far with him. He absolutely pulverizes the English language. He can't properly describe anything really. So I'm here to help you understand what's happening. To enlighten you so you can at least attempt to stay on your path. Unfortunate for me it means having to be close to you when we communicate."

"And what do they call you?"

"I'm the Keeper. I keep track of all the words that have ever been spoken between you and your Magnus."

"That reminds me, I told Magnus I'd been with some friends while the aerial was away. It's stirred some memories inside me and I'm afraid he may see something."

"Yes, I am aware of this. For now we're keeping as much as we can from the aerial, but we need to speak of these memories you're referring to. You're putting together a photo album I believe and some of those pictures are causing you to remember. Quite a good idea actually, do you understand why you need to talk about those memories?

"No. Magnus explained that I need to get them out of me."

"Of course he wouldn't be able to properly explain this either. I don't know why I even ask. Let me explain in a way you might be able to understand. Think of the aerial as having a vast library of information at his disposal, but most of it he hasn't looked at yet. When he senses something is wrong or hidden, he goes to the library and looks for it. He will eventually find what he's looking for. However, if you speak of something, then we can take it out of his library of information so he never finds it himself. This is what we must do with your cravings, your past experiences and dirty thoughts so he never sees these things. I can't believe it, but he thinks you're a sweet innocent angel! And tell me, Magnus did explain that you're not to be letting him know that you suck on the cock or that you would ever take it in your ass. Correct?

"Yes, that's correct. I've not told him of any of my sexual experiences."

"Another thing you must remember is to speak of things when they come to you because the negative will try to make you forget it all again so they can expose it to the aerial. Does this make sense?"

"Yes. I understand that better now. But how do I get a hold of you when those thoughts are coming?

"Just ask if you may speak. As our connection gets stronger, you will be able to just start speaking and those words won't go into him. This shouldn't take long for the connections to get stronger because I'll be here all the time, not like Magnus who was coming and going. Unfortunately for me, I can't leave.

"Where is Magnus?"

"He's everywhere. He's aware of everything and everything you do he sees through me. When we speak, he will know everything that we've said and when we touch, he will feel it the way I just told you. Believe me that's the one thing I'm not looking forward to."

"You're not looking forward to touching me? Why, because I have small tits?"

"I will just say this, you're not my type. I don't really see what he sees in you actually, but he keeps insisting that you're "special". I've yet to see special. Powerful One? Wet Blanket would be more like it. If I'd been him, I would have been done with you a long time ago, but oh no, your Magnus would not allow it. The only thing that saved you as far as I can tell is the fact that the other one went *sideways*. This aerial has so many different words in his head. It's refreshing after listening to Magnus for so many years. "Sideways" it is! You've got a lot of growing to do to live up to *that* name and to be any good to us. As far as I'm concerned, I don't think you're up to it."

I wonder why this energy is speaking this way to me. The feeling from Magnus has been loving and kind. He is accepting and patient with me. The

Keeper's words are otherwise to say the least and yet I don't feel a true dislike from him, sarcasm yes, but I'm not going to let him get to me. I'm surprised at my confidence in my appearance when he speaks to me. I've always been fit, well-muscled legs and buttocks, a small but rounded belly, shapely shoulders and arms, and yes small breasts, but fitting for my rather petite figure I think. My hair has been long my entire life and now the streaks of platinum draw compliments from many, mostly women. I've never had as many compliments in my entire life as I've had since being with Tom. I think it must be that people can feel my happiness and the love that surrounds me now and that's what they're attracted to it, believing it has something to do with me. Nevertheless, I feel as though I want to get closer to the Keeper, to learn and understand more rather than allow his words to hurt me. I don't think he means to be hurtful actually, but is simply being honest with me as Magnus has always been. Sometimes the truth hurts a bit, but it's still the truth.

"If you don't like me then why are you caressing my leg and touching my hair?" I ask cheekily.

"It's not me quite frankly, although it's better when we do touch because it's easier on the aerial as you know, but it's the aerial that's touching you. As I said, when he does this, we feel what he feels inside. You know when you touch yourself and it feels good inside of you? We don't feel the outside touch on your clitoris. We feel what you feel on the inside. Do you understand?"

"Yes, thank you. I do now."

"You talked earlier about the full moon. Let me explain that to you as one of your first lessons with me. Do you understand what effect the full moon has on souls?"

"Not really. I do know there's more bad things happening when there's a full moon that's for sure."

"Yes, of course. There is. When there's a full moon, the energy inside people becomes stronger. So if they're full of positive energy it makes them feel more positive about everything, about themselves and about the people around them for example. Positive feels more positive and they push that out. If they're full of negative energy they become that much more negative during the full moon and that's why you see and hear of more hell raising. It's the same force on the planet that makes the tide rise. You mentioned your patient from this day to the aerial. She's controlled by the negative now. That's why she's unable to see what she's done to her family, her children. The negative hasn't wanted her to see it because negative is feeding off her behaviour and becoming stronger as she acts more negatively. Unfortunately for her, negative doesn't quit and she will be destroyed by it. That's the feeling the negative wants and that's what she's giving them."

"What do you mean by destroyed?"

"I don't mean the end of its life, but I mean the end of what it had. She won't be able to feel what she thought was a good feeling, being with these men. What she'll feel is all this pain from what she's done to her children and to her soul mate who is a kind soul."

"That's so sad. You said good energy becomes stronger during the full moon too."

"You must remember that there's much more negative than there is positive first of all so there's a big offset. But yes, all energy is pressed down into souls more during the full moon so we become stronger also. We take advantage of the full moon. We can gather more energy during this time. You see, there's even the possibility of capturing some of the negative energy and making it positive by giving it bits of good feelings, positive feelings and if it wants more, it will eventually become more positive. Like this woman we were just talking about for example. Magnus told you words to say to her, and when you were speaking these words, were you able to convey these words to her properly? In other words, did she understand what you were saying?"

"Yes, she became angry with me."

"That is correct, she rejected them. That is the negative screaming back, saying we want nothing to do with this. Negative won out. Now she will suffer the consequences. In other words, if she had taken the words, that would be us getting more positive away from the negative, but instead she wished to stay there because she believed the negative had more to offer. Eventually she will come to realize what she has done, but it will be too late, the man that really loved her and her kids will all be gone. She will see that the ones she thought loved her were just using her. Even her friends and family will not want to be around her. Positive people, like you, do not want to be around negative and will stay away from her. That's what I mean by being destroyed."

"Thank you for explaining that to me. This is much easier for me to understand now."

"You spoke to the aerial about the young man he helped raise."

"Yes, Josh!"

"Yes, that's his name." This time we were able to help when the aerial spoke to him and much of the words went in. He allowed the words to come in and because of that, he will see the positive side and not just the negative."

"That's good news. Can you tell me more about Josh's Mom? I didn't completely understand what Magnus was saying about our paths being different because of the older ones. He also said Tom doesn't have much memory of her. Why is that?"

"Oh yes, of course a woman would want to know about the woman that preceded her. It's what you female souls are like. But this one is not one to fool with. She is still active and as you would say, dangerous."

"Dangerous?!"

"Yes, she has enough negative that she can do damage to you and your aerial's happiness. She knows what it takes to satisfy the energies."

I feel my heart starting to pound. "Will you tell me more about this and help me?"

"Yes, we will be speaking much more of this. Not only this but your future and your past as we spend time together. I'm here to keep you on your path and I will give you Clarity."


This is not the end….Clarity is coming.

# ABOUT THE AUTHOR

*"When I started to write about the fictional character called Tesh, I realized she'd always been there, within me, this playful, sensual, passionate girl who had never been allowed to surface. Telling her story has changed my life. Her fascination with men, her unabashed desires and her willingness to experience has rejuvenated me. This series, Beyond The Voices, is what I now believe to be the journey to* **Erotic Nirvana.**"

- Mary Katherine Fontanero –

Mary Katherine Fontanero is from Barcelona, Spain, where she and her husband worked as physicians. Together they travelled extensively, eventually retiring in Vancouver, Canada, where they currently reside with their dog, Sabio.

Made in the USA
San Bernardino, CA
23 August 2017